THE BOOK RACK
Thousands of Used Paperback Books
Trade or Buy 1/2 Price
8452 Watson Road
14560 Manchester Road

DOCTOR WHO
THE ROMANS

Based on the BBC television series by Dennis Spooner by arrangement with the British Broadcasting Corporation

DONALD COTTON

Number 120 in the
Doctor Who Library

A TARGET BOOK

published by
the Paperback Division of
W. H. ALLEN & Co. PLC

A Target Book
Published in 1987
by the Paperback Division of
W. H. Allen & Co. PLC
44 Hill Street, London W1X 8LB

First published in Great Britain by
W. H. Allen & Co. PLC 1987

Novelisation copyright © Donald Cotton, 1987
Original script copyright © Dennis Spooner, 1965
'Doctor Who' series copyright © British Broadcasting
Corporation, 1965, 1987

The BBC producers of *The Romans* were Verity Lambert and
Mervyn Pinfield, the director was Christopher Barry
The role of the Doctor was played by William Hartnell

Printed and bound in Great Britain by
Anchor Brendon Ltd, Tiptree, Essex

ISBN 0 426 20288 0

For Ann Wood,
With Love and Patience

This book is sold subject to the condition that it shall
not, by way of trade or otherwise, be lent,
re-sold, hired out or otherwise circulated without the
publisher's prior consent in any form of
binding or cover other than that in which it is published
and without a similar condition including this
condition being imposed on the subsequent purchaser.

CONTENTS

	Prologue	7
I	First Extract from the Journal of Ian Chesterton	11
II	First Extract from the Doctor's Diary	15
III	First Letter from Legionary (Second Class) Ascaris	19
IV	Second Extract from the Doctor's Diary	21
V	Second Extract from the Journal of Ian Chesterton	27
VI	Second Letter from Legionary (Second Class) Ascaris	31
VII	Third Extract from the Doctor's Diary	35
VIII	Third Letter from Legionary (Second Class) Ascaris	41
IX	Third Extract from the Journal of Ian Chesterton	43
X	Fourth Extract from the Doctor's Diary	45
XI	First Extract from the Commonplace Book of Poppea Sabina	49
XII	Fourth Extract from the Journal of Ian Chesterton	53
XIII	First Selection of Jottings from Nero's Scrapbook	57

XIV	Fourth Letter from Legionary (Second Class) Ascaris	61
XV	Fifth Extract from the Doctor's Diary	63
XVI	Fifth Extract from the Journal of Ian Chesterton	67
XVII	Second Extract from the Commonplace Book of Poppea Sabina	71
XVIII	A Poisoner Remembers	77
XIX	Letter from Barbara Wright	79
XX	Second Selection of Jottings from Nero's Scrapbook	81
XXI	Sixth Extract from the Journal of Ian Chesterton	89
XXII	Third Extract from the Commonplace Book of Poppea Sabina	93
XXIII	Fifth Letter from Legionary (Second Class) Ascaris	97
XXIV	Sixth Extract from the Doctor's Diary	99
XXV	Seventh Extract from the Journal of Ian Chesterton	103
XXVI	Seventh Extract from the Doctor's Diary	109
XXVII	Sixth Letter from Legionary (Second Class) Ascaris	115
XXVIII	Third Selection of Jottings from Nero's Scrapbook	117
XXIX	Eighth Extract from the Doctor's Diary	121
	Epilogue	125

PROLOGUE

Epistle to the Keeper of
the Imperial Archives, Rome

Dear Sir,

I am in reluctant receipt of your insufferable scroll – written, I must remark, on papyrus of so inferior a quality that I can only suppose it to have been selected especially to suit the style of your grammatical construction and the insolence of your tone.

One would have thought that even an Empire in Decline and Fall might have seen fit to employ a *scholar* in the august position you have the effrontery to occupy, rather than a denarius-pinching, acidulous accountant with no apparent grounding in the Humanities.

However, I realise that times are what they weren't, and that the general decline in education standards has left it likely that the technocrat shall inherit the Senate, no matter what the embitterment of the literate.

I must ask you, therefore, to attribute the fact that I now apply stylus to tablet in response – rather than inserting your impertinences into my incineratorium as they deserve – not to any old world courtesy on my part – should you be fool enough to fancy you detect any such consideration between the lines – but to the irritating circumstance that your communication is merely the latest in a dreary series of querulous queries; and I now wish to stem this nuisance at its source, before my desk becomes quite buried beneath a pile of junk mail, all of it bearing your indecipherable signature.

Now, having completed the civilities, let me at once address myself to the matter of the burden of your repetitive song.

You speak, confound you, of breach of contract; and have the further temerity to threaten the invocation of penalty clauses, if I do not at once submit for your inspection those chapters of my *Annals* which cover the Great Fire of Rome and the last few years of Nero Caesar's reign, described so aptly by my colleague Suetonius as 'The Terror'.

Now, I must make it quite clear to you that I, Tacitus, am not accustomed to being thus pestered and berated by jumped-up Iagos-in-office who are apparently incapable of recognising a hot property when they read one: for must I remind you that those sections of the book already completed have received extremely favourable advance notices from all discerning critics? And already there is talk of its dramatisation by Juvenal as the centre-piece of next year's 'Festival of Roman Arts, Culture, and Blood Sports' at the Circus Maximus.

However, since you have the infernal bad taste to speak of the possibility of your withholding not only the final down-payment, but the royalties themselves, in the event of my not delivering the goods, it seems I have no alternative but to explain the set of somewhat bizarre circumstances which have persuaded me to retain the remainder of the work – at least, until I have completed further research as to the authenticity of certain documents which have only recently come into my possession; and which would, if genuine, necessitate not only the postponement of publication, but the rewriting of History itself!

I will not detain an incompetent dunderhead like your goodself with a detailed account of how I acquired these extraordinary papers – which I now enclose for your attention. Suffice it to say that my field workers are constantly abroad about my business, and it is not for me to enquire too closely into the methods they employ in the collection of information.

It is possible, I admit, that I am in danger of becoming the victim of an elaborate hoax, devised – possibly by Suetonius – for my discomfiture. Hence my caution. But the new facts herein revealed would, if true, explain a great deal which has previously puzzled me, and I am therefore tempted to believe them.

You will remember, from your, no doubt, laborious perusal of my last manuscript, that it contains references to a series of prodigies and portents which heralded the year of the Great Fire: and that these included unnatural births, such as two-headed calves and the like; sea-monsters sporting in the Tiber; apparitions of the gibbering and squeaking, sheeted dead variety; and finally, a clutch of comets, which flamed and flared furiously over the Forum, to the horror of the opprobrious populace.

Also, unearthly noises were heard in the vicinity of Assissium: and it is my cautious submission that, for these, the enclosed exclusives may well furnish an explanation. Indeed, we would then have no choice but to believe that, during this doom-encumbered year, Rome was visited by intruders from another time, space, or similar unwelcome dimension; and that the *possibly* comet-like vehicle in which they travelled was known to them as the 'TARDIS'.

You think, perhaps, that age has at last unseated my reason, and wobbled my laurels in the process? I can only suggest that you reserve judgement until you have read the items in question; at which time it will be my dubious pleasure to receive your inept comments upon them. For the moment I will only remind you that there are more things in Olympus and Earth than are dreamed of by an urban district employee of lowly grade and status; and remain,

With marked lack of respect,

Your best-selling author of this or any other year,

Tacitus.

Post Scriptum: I have arranged these documents in what I assume to be their chronological order. You will be sensible to share this assumption.

T.

DOCUMENT I

First Extract from the Journal of Ian Chesterton

Well, we are still here, Headmaster – and, in my opinion, likely to remain so: marooned, that is to say, on an island in Time which, from all the evidence, appears to be somewhere within the dominion of Ancient Rome – though at which period in its history I am as yet unable to say. A fine thing!

Today, having nothing else to do, I returned to the wreck of the TARDIS; and, of course, found the damnable contraption much as we had left it two months ago, toppled horizontally at the bottom of a rocky ravine, and looking even more cracked and dilapidated than when Barbara and I first had the misfortune to encounter it in I. M. Foreman's junk yard.

However, I was alarmed to see that yet another tree had fallen across it, and that much of its battered exterior is now obscured by a grasping growth of brambles and other hardy perennials, making it difficult for me to believe that the machine can ever be extricated from its present predicament; or indeed, that if restored to the vertical, it will ever again be functional, even in its habitual haphazard fashion.

I was nevertheless making a lonely and hopeless attempt at defoliation when a restraining hand was placed on my shoulder, causing me to leap into a nettle-bed, and a petulant voice demanded that I desist . . .

'My dear Chesterton,' exclaimed the Doctor, 'whatever are you about? That vegetation provides a valuable camouflage against the prying eyes of the curious! Would you wish the TARDIS to be discovered and our secret revealed?'

'I can't see that it really makes much odds,' I told him. 'As far as I'm concerned, anyone can find it and welcome for all the good it's likely to do them. Can you seriously believe that God's gift to industrial archeology will ever get off the ground again?'

He chuckled, in that irritating way of his. 'In N-dimensional space, dear boy, the ground, as you call it, is an out-dated concept with no relevance whatever to our momentary mechanical malfunction, or our temporary temporal predicament . . . '

'And what about our human predicament? How are we going to get out of here?'

'Please! There is no cause for alarm. The TARDIS would function just as well as always . . . '

'That is simply not good enough!'

'*I* am speaking, Chesterton. Just as well as always, I say, were it to be inverted in an erupting volcanic crater or rotating at the centre of a cyclone. Its environment is in no sense germane to its interior.'

'A great comfort! So how do you suggest we *penetrate*

its interior to find out if you're right or not? There's a hulking great tree trunk blocking the door! Here – give me a hand, can't you?'

'All in good time, my dear Chesterton. For one thing, I am *invariably* right . . . and, in any case, there is surely no hurry, is there? For once, I advise you to relax, and enjoy a short holiday. Personally I'm having a marvellous time . . . '

And do you know, Headmaster, I really believe he meant it? Producing a bunch of grapes, he offered me a couple; and then, cackling maniacally, he trotted off, looking for all the world like Bacchus on his way to an informal debauch! Sometimes I begin to believe that the man is demented!

For moreover – yet another instance, here – on my returning to the villa which has become our bivouac, I discovered that, incredibly, he has allowed Barbara and Vicki to wander off to the local town unaccompanied – to do, he says, some shopping! How about that? *Which* local town? He fails to remember, so I cannot even follow them. He has no sense of responsibility whatever; and once more I can only regret the impulse of misguided curiosity which first led me to become entangled in his eccentric, tortuous, and altogether incomprehensible affairs.

Or rather, which *will* one day lead me to become so entangled; for, since we have been travelling *backwards* in time, I suppose I haven't met him yet. How very difficult this all is! Well, in that case, when I *do* meet him for the first time, I shall do my utmost not to recognise him, and see how he likes that!

Meanwhile, all I can usefully do it seems, is to continue to record events in this journal; in the hope that one day in some unimaginably distant future it will enable you, Headmaster, and the school governors, of course, to realise that your science master has been trapped by history, and your history mistress snared by science; instead of your continuing to believe, as you doubtless do, that Barbara and I have eloped together!

For it is my constant fear that unless I can somehow dispel this not unnatural suspicion, it could well lead to the forfeit of our potential pensions, and then where would we be? And where are we now, come to that? I wish I knew; but meanwhile remain,

Your always loyal employee,
Ian Chesterton.

DOCUMENT II

First Extract from the Doctor's Diary

I am becoming increasingly worried about young Chesterton – if that *is* his name. For some time now he has been morose and unco-operative, but today has added tantrums and sulks to these melancholy qualities, and I begin to fear that his disaffection, if unchecked, may well have a deleterious effect on morale. It is almost as if he were not enjoying the unique experience of exploring time and space which I, at some personal inconvenience and to the detriment of my own weightier affairs, have been able to provide for him.

Well, to be honest, it is in fact convenient for me to slip from circulation for a small sabbatical until, as they say, the heat is off: but nevertheless Chesterton's constant nonsense about returning to the singularly uncivilised century, where I found him, is irritating, to say the least. One would have thought that even the merest glimpse of the grandeur that is Rome – if I may coin a phrase? – would have been sufficient to persuade him that life under the Emperors is infinitely preferable to the squalor that was England in 1963!

Enough of this. I am not to be diverted from my primary purposes by the witless whims of a secondary school master; and, in view of his behaviour, I have decided that on no account can he be allowed to accompany me to Rome itself – for that is where I intend to go as soon as I have completed my arrangements for the journey. Besides, his fashionable passion for so-called democracy might have been all very well during the Republic, but could hardly fail to raise eyebrows and attract attack in the Empire. Suppose, for instance, that he were to advocate its transformation into a Commonwealth? No, it would never do – as it never does, in my experience.

Further, and after some reflection, I have also decreed that Barbara Wright shall remain here with him. She and Vicki have just returned from what I intended to have been a cautious reconnaissance foray to the neighbouring market town, and what do I find? Why, that instead of sounding the ground as instructed, they have attracted undesirable attention to themselves by what I can only describe as an unauthorised orgy of public spending, and purchased enough drapery, napery, and similar feminine fal-lals as to overstock the bargain basement of a consumerama!

Mind you, I do not blame Vicki for this. She is a sensible child; and has never to my knowledge previously been exposed to the compulsive unnecessary expenditure syndrome on which capitalist society is so ludicrously based. So she shall certainly be allowed to be my travelling companion and confidante during the enterprise.

Already, it seems, she has discovered that the present Caesar is the Emperor Nero: and I am convinced that a glimpse of his artistic and cultural achievements will prove to be not only educational but positively stimulating for her.

For my part, I would certainly like to interview the man, for I have always suspected that History has dealt harshly with him. For instance, I have never believed that he fiddled during the famous conflagration; and I base this conclusion on the fact that the violin had not as yet been invented; no, the instrument, if any, must surely have been a lyre. So, if the fiddle be myth, then what of the Great Fire itself? Well, we shall see – for no doubt Nero himself will be able to enlighten me in due course . . .

Later: hardly had I written the above, when Vicki provided an instant corroboration of my musical speculations.

It appears that, this very morning, she and Barbara encountered in town a quavering ancient who professed himself to be a wandering scholar or bard; and who proceeded to prove this contention for the benefit of such passers-by as he could detain, by the performance of a rambling iambic account of the Rape of Lucretia.

Hardly a suitable subject for a mixed audience, I would have thought; but no matter: the important point is that he accompanied this piece of prurient scurrility upon an instrument which can only have been – from Vicki's description – a lyre!

So I was right – as always! What a bright child she is, to be sure! And what an amenable amanuensis she will make during my short survey of the foundations of Western Culture . . .

We shall leave for Rome tomorrow.

DOCUMENT III

First Letter from Legionary (Second Class) Ascaris

Salve, Mater!

I hope you are well as habitual, and as it leaves me also, I am pleased to say.

Well, this new posting is a piece of cake and cushy as they come, so do not worry or fret as I would have expected of you if I'd been sent to bash barbarians in Gaul like my poor eagle-carrying mates.

So, guess what! I have been taken off normal duties, and put on special service to the Empire! So how about that for a bit of all right, eh? What it boils down to, though, is that I am at this moment sitting in a bush waiting to kill a lyre-player – or should that be lyricist? Anyway, it's a fact, and one on account of which I could not be happier, neither of my ears being in the least musical, as you and Dad have reason enough to know I should think! Well, you can't have everything, can you? But what I do have is these other homicidal tendencies, which were once a worry to you, but can now be put to good use at the Emperor's pleasure. For the whisper in the barracks is that my orders come from his very self, the crack-brained twit!

And why, you may ask, should His Imperial Obesity concern himself over the disembowelment of one humble musician, when there are so many other more distinguished persons nearer home who are simply asking for it, many of them relatives, and at least one his wife?

Well, I will tell you: it appears that this particular target is by no means humble, but reckoned to be in the running for the Golden Rose Bowl at the Senate Song Contest for which you will have seen the publicity hand-outs in full colour. And, of course, His Nibs can't have that, can he? 'Cause he's already tagged the trophy for his own purposes, and moreover cleared a space for it on his dining table.

So what I'm required to do is nobble the favourite, thank you, and sharp about it, or else! Would you ever believe artistic licence could go so far? Never mind, I anticipate no difficulty, as they tell me the jazz-singer in question is of an elderly type and not likely to put up much of a struggle.

Must close now, as I think I see the innocent victim approaching down the Assissium Road, and I have to get my dagger drawn, et cetera.

But will let you know how things turn out in my next.

Till then I can only remain,

Your unusual but affectionate son,
Ascaris.

DOCUMENT IV

Second Extract from the Doctor's Diary

Vicki and I set out for Rome this morning with a brisk step and high hearts; for there is nothing, to my mind, more calculated to bring a spring to the leg muscles and a tone to the torso than the prospect of a day or two spent in the exploration of ancient monuments and the deciphering of hieroglyphics; followed, as I hope, by an evening or so in the company of one of the most unscrupulous and blood-soaked tyrants in History!

What an unrivalled cultural opportunity I am providing for the child, as I keep explaining to her. Why this should be *necessary* I do not know, but I suppose her somewhat subdued manner to be occasioned by the temporary but unavoidable separation from her two refractory friends, Ian and Barbara, of whom she appears to be quite fond.

I must say that the latter have hidden their disappointment at being excluded from the expedition with well-simulated equanimity; but I am not so easily deceived, and am confident that this relatively brief period of being, as it were, confined to barracks will prove to be a salutary lesson for them. As we left they were breakfasting *al fresco* in the rose arbour by the ornamental lake, affecting to enjoy some silly syllabub or other, washed down with some rather inferior local wine, and pretended not to notice our departure. No doubt words failed them – a disability from which, mercifully, I have never suffered; and I was still chuckling at my small disciplinary triumph when Vicki and I refreshed ourselves at the roadside with some really delicious crab-apples, ripe as they would ever be, and a bowl or so of only slightly sulphurous pond-water; in which I admit I detected, almost too late, the remains of a somewhat anaemic frog or toad.

Since these raddled remnants first manifested themselves in Vicki's portion, I was at first inclined to attribute her expression of frozen horror to that circumstance – for she is sometimes over-squeamish in dietary matters – but on following the direction indicated by her quivering forefinger, I observed an upturned and blood-stained human foot protruding from the thorny undergrowth in which we had hitherto been relaxing. Her subsequent scream was, in these circumstances, quite understandable, and I therefore saw fit not to rebuke the girl.

A cautious examination proved the foot to be attached to the leg of an emaciated *corpus delicti*, detectably done to death by a knife which still protruded from the rib-cage, and probably, I deduced, the victim of some rogue or foot-pad; such as, I now remembered, were a notorious hazard in the Italian hinterland at this time, and I therefore resolved to keep a sharp look-out in the future.

The body was that of an elderly man, whose fine, distinguished, intellectual features somewhat resembled my own: and it was to this coincidence that I at first attributed Vicki's claim that she recognised him.

'Nonsense,' I said, 'how could you? But if you inspect him closely, you will see that he and I have several points in common, prominent amongst which are the handsome, aristocratic face, and the long sensitive hands. It is this which has misled you.'

She gave me a look which under other circumstances I would have described as impertinent, but no doubt she was still *distraite* from her discovery, so I overlooked the matter.

'I tell you, Barbara and I saw him in the market only yesterday,' she said; 'and, if you remember, I told you so at the time. It's the lyre-player who sang that embarrassing song about Lucretia! Very vulgar, it was!'

I agreed that, on second thoughts, the resemblance was not so strong as I had supposed; for I now noticed a lubricious curl defacing the dead lips, which I had hitherto taken to be a symptom of the death-agony. But I was still not altogether convinced by her identification, for surely a lyre-player might reasonably be expected to carry a lyre about him?

'He was. You've been sitting on it for the last twenty minutes,' she informed me; somewhat pertly, I fancied.

'In that case, why didn't you say so at once?' I demanded, rising to inspect the instrument, which I had hitherto taken to be one of those superannuated bedsteads so commonly discarded in places designated as being of special scenic interest. 'I might have damaged it.'

'It sounds as if you have,' she said, plucking a tentative A-string, which emitted a feline whine.

'Give it to me!' I told her; somewhat impatiently perhaps, for it seems to me that her remarks sometimes teeter on the edge of criticism. 'The instrument only needs to be tuned . . . '

'Go on, then,' she said; 'I suppose you'll tell me you're a professional lyre-tuner next?'

'I am naturally acquainted with the basic principles of harmonics,' I informed her, stiffly, 'as indeed with all scientific matters . . . '

And I was proceeding to investigate the dynamics of the apparatus, when my attention was drawn to a Roman centurion who had approached us unobserved; and who was now slashing savagely about the bushes with a sword of sorts, an expression of vexed perplexity on his forbidding features.

'Have a care there, my good fellow!' I advised him, not wishing him to discover the deceased and assume us responsible for its current condition. 'You are damaging your valuable botanical heritage . . . '

'Damaging my what?' he enquired suspiciously.

'Viper's bugloss,' I informed him. 'These plants are not common in the Mediterranean eco-system . . . ' A remark which gave him the pause I had anticipated, and of which I took advantage to ask if he'd lost something.

'Well, I thought I had,' he replied, approaching us with the measured tread which had already carried the *Pax Romana* so far afield; 'but I seem to have found it, after all . . .'

He looked at the lyre in my hands, with what I can only describe as angry incredulity. 'Forgive me,' he said, 'but am I, by any chance, addressing Maximus Petullian, the celebrated Corinthian ballad-monger, whose melodies have set a nation's feet a-tapping?'

Rather to Vicki's astonishment, I fancy, I decided to adopt the pseudonym so conveniently proffered. The question of my identity has often been a difficult one to resolve during my travels.

'Precisely!' I told him. 'I am flattered to find that my reputation has arrived ahead of me . . .'

'Oh, indeed,' he confirmed; 'and our meeting is therefore a most happy coincidence. Our Emperor was most concerned to learn that you had decided to *walk* to Rome, giving impromptu folk-recitals on the road; and he has sent me to give you safe conduct to the court. He is greatly looking forward to discussing with you the state of modern music, and would not wish to be disappointed in this by the circumstances of your death and mutilation by anti-social elements. You haven't, I suppose,' he continued thoughtfully, 'already been attacked by any of the latter? Such as legionary, second class, Ascaris, for instance? I only mention the name because he is a refractory fellow with strongly critical ideas on the art of fugue, which have disrupted many a regimental sing-song. Also he is known to be in the district. He once eviscerated a harpist,' he amplified, 'so I thought I'd better ask . . .'

I pointed out that my own viscera were still manifestly *in situ*; and with many a jocular expression of relief at this happy state of affairs, we continued in company on the road to Rome.

But, for some reason, I do not altogether trust the man, and I shall watch him closely . . .

DOCUMENT V

Second Extract from the Journal of Ian Chesterton

Should I ever be so unfortunate as to encounter the Doctor again, I shall try to redeem the occasion by telling him just what I think of his complacent incompetence, and its relevance to the apparently hopeless situation in which I now find myself.

Brilliant scientist as debatably he may be – at least in his own frequently expressed opinion – he appears to have less sense of the practical realities of life than the average ineducable fourth form drop-out, and about as much mental stability as a . . . as a . . . But why should I grope for a suitable simile, when such a meeting becomes increasingly unlikely? Nor can I bring myself to think that I shall ever again see my friend and colleague, Barbara Wright, whose well meant assistance has led to my present predicament; but no matter what the obstacles I must try to find her somehow, for her own situation can scarcely be better, and is probably even worse than my own.

Let me try to put events into some sort of rational order while I still have a clear mind; and indeed, the strength to do so, for I fear I cannot survive much more of this!

'Of what?' you ask, Headmaster, with your quite understandable end of term brusqueness? All in good time, I promise you – but first you must permit me a preamble, or you will be lost in the convolutions of the subsequent narrative.

Hardly had the Doctor and Vicki departed on their ill-advised expedition, when two strangers arrived at the villa. I regarded them with some apprehension; for in spite of the Doctor's confident assertion that the owners of the property are obviously on an extended vacation, I have never been happy in my mind about the terms of our dubious tenancy, and have been awaiting the return of the ground landlords with an anxiety not unmixed with a tendency to jump like a jerboa at noises in the night.

However, although rather rough-looking, the newcomers addressed us in a civil enough manner, asking if our holocaust – I *think* that's what they said – if our holocaust was functioning effectively; being, they claimed, from the under-floor heating maintenance department in Assissium.

We assured them that since the installation of the system we had used no other; having, in fact, even gone so far as to tell our friends about it. And this having been established to their satisfaction, we invited them to join us in a goblet or so of Samian wine, for it was a warm day; and they accepted with what appeared to be pleasure.

Oh, why did it not occur to me then, Headmaster, that on a warm day the heating apparatus might reasonably have been expected to be off? But you can't think of everything, can you?

For a while the conversation circled round various small-talk and gossip topics, such as the inadequate provision of bread and circuses by the municipal authorities; and whether in our opinion, they wondered, Nero really *had* killed his mother. Things like that. And then, out of the blue, the elder of the two – Sevcheria by name – asked Barbara if she had any news at all from Londinium these days?

She had the quick wit and intelligence to look blank – for which I gave her full marks – and, adopting a mentally retarded expression, asked him why he should ever suppose such a thing?

At this the younger, and obviously subordinate artisan – one Didius – grinned offensively – mind you, he'd had a couple by then – tapped his nose with a grimy forefinger, and said that she and her pretty little friend – yes, and where was *she*, by the way? – had not only made a generally favourable impression on the market traders of Assissium yesterday, but had incautiously enquired the current exchange rate as between pounds and lira, when purchasing a dress-length of white samite (Oh, mystic, wonderful, Barbara!) in the shopping precinct. So come on, now – they *were* Britons, weren't they? Natives of that off-shore island where the good times are, and the girls know a thing or two, ha, ha!

I groaned inwardly – feeling that an outward manifestation of my horror at their indiscretion would serve no useful purpose at this time – and tried unsuccessfully to kick Barbara on the ankle; unfortunately knocking

Sevcheria's stool from beneath him in the process. At this he drew himself up to his full height, albeit with some difficulty, produced from beneath his toga one of those nasty looking, twisted daggers that Arabs use in films – you must have seen them – and said that if that was the way I wanted it, I could have it, and welcome!

I was still considering the implications of this, when Didius seized Barbara by the arm, and giggling suggestively, opined that she was certainly going to fetch a good price at the slave-sales in Rome: from which I deduced, correctly as it transpires, that these men were, in fact, slave traders, and not heating engineers at all, as they had deceptively claimed!

I acted on the instant, and leaped – from a sitting position, I ask you to note! – at Sevcheria's knees, in the sort of tackle with which I once brought down the Old Boys' wing three-quarter at a critical moment in the game (you will, no doubt, recall the occasion), but unfortunately at the same time Barbara aimed a blow at Didius' head with an empty wine-jar, which coincided with my own athletic trajectory, and knocked me cold, thereby frustrating my initiative!

I knew no more until I regained my senses chained to a bench in what I can only assume to be a war-galley of Nero's battle-fleet, a coarse voice enquiring if I felt better now, because if so perhaps I would care to join my fellow oarsmen in a little healthy exercise?

It is now, thank God, the coffee break; and I take this first opportunity of informing you, Headmaster, of the reason for my continued absence.

With my best wishes as always,

Ian Chesterton.

DOCUMENT VI

Second Letter from
Legionary (Second Class) Ascaris

Well, here I am again, Mater,

So please forgive writing, grammar, and punctuation as always. I said in my last that I would let you know at my soonest how things turned out with respect to the ambush of the lyre-player, Maximus Petullian; but I now find some difficulty in acquainting you with same, as I am no longer sure of the facts, and am beginning to doubt my sanity in consequence.

Yes, I know you have often kindly warned me of the danger of losing my reason if I carried on the way I was, but I no longer do so recently, and this is something else again, as I'm sure you will agree when I tell you, which I will now embark upon.

Listen: you will remember with pride, I am sure, as how I was about to leap from hiding upon that misbegotten minstrel with dagger drawn and teeth bared et cetera? Right? Right! So this I proceeded to do, with all the ferocity at my disposal, which as per usual is considerable when roused, taking the poor old party round the throat with one hand while slipping my knife between his spare ribs with another; at which he forthwith died, with a most unmusical gurgle which was a pleasure to hear. I then concealed his remains in the shrub which I had recently vacated, leaving the instrument of death – as we call it, in the trade – protruding from his chest as instructed, so as to indicate to any interested prod-nose persons that Vandals were the cause, and by no means yours truly, Ascaris of the Ninth, which would never do.

So then, conscious of a job well done in all particulars, I left the bleeding remains to get on with it, and took myself off to a nearby tavern, there to report events to my superior officer, and receive any further instructions and/or praise which might be going. Whereupon, somewhat to my only very natural resentment, I should think, he declared in that classical Latin voice of his which always gets up my nostrils, that he'd best go and see for himself before handing out the rewards of merit, and off he forthwith popped.

Left to myself, I went into the bar – yes, I know what you've told me, but can't you understand how I could truly do with a drop after my recent traumatic experience? For although killing is my second nature, it is my first – failed candidate for the priesthood, simply because I couldn't handle the Hebrew, I ask you! – which has to be subdued on these *post mortem* occasions, and I find alcohol an admirable specific to this end, don't I?

I was therefore entertaining the dwindling company to my generally admired rendition of the Second Ode of Horace, Book Three, when my shoulder sagged beneath the weight of a centurion's hand.

'Well, Ascaris,' says he; 'enjoying yourself, are you?'

I admitted that, for the nonce, I was indeed seeing the Roman World through rose-coloured retinas, and I invited him to join me in this enterprise, but he would have none of it. No: slapping me about the face with a metal-studded gauntlet, he asks, polite as you please, if I can refresh instead his memory as to where exactly I have dumped the deceased.

'Why,' I told him, spitting out a tooth for which I had no further use, 'in the shade of an old apple tree, or some such. Last on the right as you go towards Assissium. If you start from here, that is . . . '

'Then how is it,' he enquired, in a voice throbbing, like they say with menace, 'that the late-lamented blood-soaked victim, having cleaned the scarlet stains of your brutal assault off his toga, has just booked in to the first floor back of this select, grade twelve establishment? Answer me that, if you will be so very kind!' Whereupon he once more swats me, this time in the bread-basket.

Partly because of this, I was not at once able to furnish an explanation, as you can well imagine. But in any case, I mean, well, look here, the time has been, as someone says somewhere, that the dead would lie where left. But now apparently the yawning graves yield their ghastly inmates, to push us from our bar stools. Which eventually, having got my breath back where it belonged, I said so, but he was not obviously impressed by such impromptu rhetoric; and has since told me that if I wish to rise, however eventually, to Legionary First Class, I must finish the job so ill-begun, this very evening. Which I now propose to attempt – but with what qualms of a morbidly superstitious nature I can only leave you to improvise.

I didn't join for this, as I need hardly say, but will have another murderous go as requested, and let you know what happens *this* time . . .

Am going to have just one for the road, and then be about it.

In haste,

Your disturbed son,
Ascaris.

PS. Why did you and Dad name me after a parasitic worm? Always meant to ask . . .

DOCUMENT VII

Third Extract from The Doctor's Diary

A disturbed night, as I was intelligent enough to anticipate, and therefore on the 'qui-vive?'

After some reflection I had decided not to share with Vicki my suspicions about our travelling companion, considering that recent events – which included bodies in bushes and toads in bowls, you will recall – might possibly have unhinged her tiny mind sufficiently for one day.

I therefore advised her to take early retirement, and soothed her indignant objections by pointing out that the morrow's programme not only included a long and arduous forced march through difficult and dangerous terrain, but the possibility of lethal assault by the maniac, Ascaris, of whom the suspect centurion had been thoughtful enough to warn us.

I fancy this comforted her to some extent; and she went obediently to her room, muttering something inaudible in which I could only detect the words 'senile dementia' – possibly a reference to the late Maximus Petullian, though on what grounds she should doubt his sanity I am unable to say – and with only the evidence of a light pallor about her features to indicate that I was right to surmise that she had allowed herself to become over-tired. Youth is so often unaware of the physical limitations which the more mature have learnt to take in their stride; as indeed I always ignore my own, if any.

After a pleasant hour or so spent in lecturing my new military acquaintance on the relative advantages and disadvantages of the phalanx and tortudo when campaigning against Parthian cavalry – a subject on which I consider myself to be something of an expert – I noticed that he was beginning to display signs of drowsiness, and took this as the cue to plead my own fatigue – simulated, needless to say – and go to my quarters; for I deemed it prudent to get in a little lyre practice, if I were to be able to converse with Nero about the instrument on anything like an equal footing.

I soon mastered the rudimentary principles on which the lyre can be persuaded to operate, and was endeavouring to implement some permutations which had occurred to me involving its more advanced harmonic frequencies, when I was distracted from this pleasant pastime by a series of thumps and bangs, which appeared to emanate from the next room.

My immediate impression was that my neighbour might possibly be a percussion player, anxious to accompany my impromptu recital; and glad as always to accept professional assistance whenever offered, I strode rapidly to the communicating door, which I flung open with a few well-chosen words of welcome, which now escape me. But no matter; for it was soon obvious that for once I was under a misapprehension.

Crouched in the centre of the room, beating on the floor with his simian fists, his already unappealing features contorted further by an expression of malign fury which temporarily obscured his eyes in rolls of fat, or some such substance, was a squat figure in the uniform of a Legionary, second class; which on the self-same instant sprang headlong through the space where the door had been until I opened it; and carried by its own inept impetus across the width of my own accommodation, it presently came to rest in a crumpled heap at the foot of the opposite wall, where it lay, breathing deeply, and gloomily inspecting a severe laceration of the left hand caused by a knife grasped in the right.

'Damn!' it complained loudly; but in so slurred a voice that I had no difficulty in coming to the conclusion that the man was not only on a murderous errand, but at least partially intoxicated! And since it seemed to me that it could only have been my 'prentice performance on the lyre which had roused him to this paranoid pitch, a moment's further thought inclined me to the belief that this creature must certainly be that self-same Ascaris about whose homicidal musical criticism I had already been apprised.

It was therefore but the work of a further moment for me to entangle his flailing limbs in a blanket which I snatched, toreador-like from my bed; and then to rain a series of stinging blows about his bestial body.

(I was once, as is well known, a highly-rated practitioner of pugilism and other martial arts.)

Ignoring his agonised cries of 'Gerroff!', I now proceeded to entwine the strings of my instrument about his cloven fists, from one of which I then had no difficulty in removing the knife; and victory was mine!

I hauled him to his feet, and was about to question him closely as to his murderous activities, when the door behind me opened once more, this time to admit my young friend Vicki; who misinterpreting as always the essence of the situation, screamed so loudly as to startle me. Whereupon I fear I jumped, and inadvertently pushed my assailant out through the window, before I could obtain the information from him which I required.

It seems likely that he then escaped into the night, for there was no sign of his mangled remains when I remembered to look this morning.

Breakfast was a gloomy meal; for I am, I must say, becoming irritated by Vicki's constant juvenile and hysterical intrusions into my masterly grasp of affairs, and next time I think I may well leave her at home, or at least in the TARDIS.

Conversation was, therefore, sporadic; and not much enlivened by the centurion's naive, and, it seemed to me, *nervous* attempts to question me: 'Had I really slept all *that* well?' 'Was I absolutely positive that my privacy had *not* been invaded during the night by some kill-crazed assassin or other?' And much more to the same effect.

I answered all these questions with the dismissive, absent-minded smile I keep for such occasions, and turned to my devilled kidneys and kedgeree in the confident knowledge that I was right, as ever, not to trust the man. He knows more than he admits: and in spite of his over-bland protestations of friendship, I now believe him to be in league with the villain!

Never mind: today we shall be in Rome – where I am confident I shall find an opponent more worthy of my steel: namely the Emperor Nero!

DOCUMENT VIII

Third Letter from
Legionary (Second Class) Ascaris

Dear Mum,

How would you and Dad feel about buying me out of the legion, and the sooner the better? I have made enquiries, and find that by a happy coincidence the sum required is exactly equal to your life savings, and would be money well-spent in my opinion.

I will not trouble you with all the details which have led me to decide on a change of career, but execution comes into it, and I naturally don't want that at my age.

I have no fixed address at the moment, but a reply dropped down the first grating of the main sewer, just after it leaves the Temple of Minerva, is almost certain to reach me, if you follow?

Wish you were here.

Oh, and please keep the news that I am back in Rome to yourself for the present, and oblige

Your undone son,
Ascaris

DOCUMENT IX

Third Extract from the Journal of Ian Chesterton

To think that in my previous existence I should ever have contemplated spending a summer holiday cruising these turbulent waters, the tempestuous reality of which is so very different from what the travel brochures lead one to expect! I have yet to see a sunlit vista, and pine-capped promontories escape me.

Instead, the restricted visibility offered by the neighbouring slimy and barnacle encrusted oar-port affords me a cheerless view in which rotten rocks and an apparently bottomless swirling vortex feature prominently – Scylla, possibly, and Charybdis, perhaps; but I fear I have neglected my classical studies in favour of scientific principles; and a fat lot of good those are at the moment, I must say! Archimedes' hare-brained hypothesis provides no comfort whatsoever in my present situation. In fact, I would rather *not* know what volume of water is likely to be displaced by a falling body; since I gather from the galley-master that the body in question is likely to be my own, if I do not make even more strenuous efforts to synchronise my strokes with those of my fellow oarsmen.

The tyrant in question is a sadistic brute of no perceptible intellectual endowment, whose goodwill I have forfeited by a vain attempt to bring him low by another of my rugger tackles. I was, of course, hampered in this endeavour by the safety-belt of salt-corroded iron which secures me to my seat; but the obscene expression which escaped his lips when I later cracked him across the shin with a water-cask warned me at once that these solo escape attempts are probably misguided and doomed to failure. But escape I must if I am ever to rescue Barbara from whatever unthinkable fate awaits her in the Roman slave-market, and I therefore need an accomplice.

To this end I have made the acquaintance of my colleague on the thwart, a giant, bearded Greek called Delos, who claims to have been a winner of the Pentathlon at Olympus in his youth.

As I myself have some small experience as a deputy games master at Coal Hill – you may remember, Headmaster, that I took over at a moment's notice when Farthingale lost an ear during a hockey scrimmage? – I fancy that together we shall be able to give a good account of ourselves, should fortune favour us with an opportunity to strike back at the beastly bully. But I confess I do not quite see how such an occasion can possibly arise; for since my last ill-fated attempt the man appears to be very much on his guard, and has – quite literally – the whip hand! Thank God for a sense of humour!

To add to our discomfort, the weather has worsened even while I have been writing this: and am I right in recollecting from my somewhat scant knowledge of Ancient History that, on one occasion, Nero's entire battle-fleet foundered when almost in sight of Ostia? If so, then I fear that I may well drown before I have a chance to be born; and in that case you, Headmaster, will never have a junior member of staff called,

Sincerely,
Ian Chesterton.

PS. If you have not, then please disregard this letter.

DOCUMENT X

Fourth Extract from The Doctor's Diary

Another myth exploded! Not all roads lead to Rome by any means, and Vicki and I have had much ado to find the place: our false friend and guide, the centurion, having left the tavern whilst I was still busy with breakfast, without saying goodbye, and without, as I later discovered, troubling to settle his account with the management! Is this an example of the Stoical Roman Virtue one hears so highly praised?

I was thus under the necessity of paying for *three* rooms, et cetera, in order to redeem my lyre from the proprietress, who remarked nastily that she had met my sort before. I believe her to be mistaken in this, but was naturally in no position to argue, and I find the whole episode outrageous! Should we meet the man again I shall certainly speak to him extremely sharply; and if he is unwilling to repay his debt to me, then I must seriously consider reporting his behaviour to the Emperor, whose emissary he claims to be.

However, after many an irritating detour, we eventually achieved the Appian Way; and after this had little difficulty in reaching the City itself, except for that occasioned by dodging the racing wheels of several chariot squadrons, whose drivers appeared to have little or no road sense – or patience either, come to that, since they continually lashed out at each other with horse-whips in what seemed to me to be a thoroughly indisciplined manner, and with small regard for the convenience of pedestrians. Here is another circumstance which I must certainly bring to Nero's attention at the earliest opportunity, for such behaviour can only have an adverse effect on the Empire's reputation for 'gravitas'.

But what of Rome itself? I am prepared to allow that it cannot have been built in a day, since there is such a lot of it; but feel that it will probably be improved by the lapse of a few more centuries, when the popular mellowing effect of Time may have reduced the somewhat Cyclopean modern architecture to a more picturesquely ruinous condition, compatible with a melancholy mourning for departed glories and vanished splendours. At the moment it is brash, to say the least!

High-rise temples, where priests ponder their impenetrable penetralia, impossibly jostle with unimaginably impractical palaces, fumbling for a foothold amongst a crawling sprawl of tenebrous tenements; inimical, I would say, to any proper sense of community in the populace, who seem for the most part an ill-kempt lot and ripe for revolution, if the Prætorian Guards were prepared to let them get on with it!

Wishing to purchase provisions for my importunate young protegée, I asked one of the latter if he could direct us to the market place; and having unscrambled his patronising ablative absolutes and plumbed his disgruntled gerundives, we came at length to an amenity area where some kind of an auction was about to begin. However, it soon became apparent that we were in the wrong department, for not a vegetable was on display: and, on consulting the auctioneer, a drunken functionary named Sevcheria, I quickly realised that we had unwittingly stumbled into the slave market. Not wishing Vicki to witness so degrading a spectacle, I was hustling her towards the exit – none too gently, I fear – when the slaves themselves, those wretched victims of an outworn social system, were paraded onto a platform, and the bidding started.

One of them, a really quite handsome but woebegone young woman, bore some slight resemblance to Barbara – although the latter, I am sure, would never have consented to appear in public in so dishevelled a condition! However, the similarity was sufficient to give me further cause for self-congratulation that I had had the wisdom to leave Miss Wright at the villa, where she can come to no possible harm.

The slave-girl appeared to sense my interest, and waved at me frantically; but I nevertheless rejected Sevcheria's insulting invitation to make him an offer for the poor woman; and before hurrying out after Vicki, I saw her purchased by a really ill-favoured fellow who gave his name as Tavius. I shudder to imagine what her future life will be like in the service of such a creature!

I have made a note to take up the case of all such unfortunates, as soon as I am alone with Nero . . .

DOCUMENT XI

First Extract from the Commonplace Book of Poppea Sabina

Do I really *like* being Empress of Rome, I wonder? Of course, it *does* make me the richest and most influential woman in the whole known world, and that is *something*, I suppose. But we have to set against it the fact that the one *essential* qualification for the job is that I be married to the Emperor – and Nero is *zero*, in every sense of the word!

Oh, what a fool I was to allow myself to be wooed and won by all that romantic nonsense he gave me about having just poisoned his mother! Because he didn't even do *that* himself – no, he left the whole business to Locusta as usual – and even then it seems that the old battle-axe had to be finished off with blunt instruments after she swam ashore from the funeral barge!

Just big talk, that's all it was – lover's lies to turn a young girl's head; but innocent as I am, I trusted him, and now there's no way out but the vein in the bath or the asp in the bosom, and I don't fancy that, thank you!

Unless . . . unless I get *him* first, of course . . . But, heigh-ho, these are only idle dreams, for I am but a poor weak woman with only one pair of hands, and must leave all that kind of rough stuff to some disaffected officer or other. How fortunate that most of the Household Cavalry are my lovers, and prepared to do anything for me, on the usual terms.

Well, we shall just have to see how my whimsy wafts me – but a regular old butcher's shop of an assassination, like when Uncle Caligula got *his* . . . That would be fun now, wouldn't it?

But I mustn't ramble artlessly on like this, because there is a more immediate problem which distracts me. For some time I have been aware that Nero has been recruiting into my personal retinue of hand-maidens, slaves of a more than usual comeliness, and I suspect his motives. Can he be planning to deceive me with one, or all of them? Would he dare? And has he the strength?

Another one arrived this morning, introduced into my quarters by the cretinous and altogether loathsome Tavius, the palace staff-gatherer; a man whose very presence fills me with the sort of nausea I normally reserve for my husband. The girl was obviously so overjoyed to be released from the clutches of this unpleasant excrescence that she appeared to accept the conditions of service – namely, death on departure, and no nonsense about days off – without demur, and only the smallest, barely perceptible shudder. But I wonder . . . There is a look about her of suppressed resentment, which might well mature to mutiny, given half a chance. And her name, which is Barbara, has – well – Barbarian overtones, so to speak.

I was mulling over these and related matters, whilst simultaneously instructing her in her duties, when Nero entered the room on the pretext of wishing to speak to me. But as usual he had nothing to say, and merely sat there, idly flicking a frenetic plectrum across his lyre with such petulance as to snap the G-string.

In itself this might have been nothing. However, since the catastrophe occurred as he was regarding Barbara with a look of licentious lasciviousness on his fat features I could only suppose the incidents to be somehow related.

My suspicions were almost immediately confirmed, when on my sending the girl from the room with a tray of tea-things, he made some spurious excuse about feeling a poem coming on, and followed her into the corridor. Only seconds later my ears were pierced by the crashing of smashed crockery and a semi-stifled scream. I glanced rapidly after them to find the girl had disappeared about her business, leaving my husband ankle-deep in fragments of priceless Etruscan cups; which, on becoming conscious of my presence, he tried vainly to conceal beneath the hem of his toga. In one hand he held a dented tray, and in the other a bent buttered scone; and, alas, 'twas with the latter that he attempted to blow me an ingratiating kiss, to the ludicrous detriment of that gesture.

But in any case, I am no longer to be disarmed by such elephantine gallantry.

Was ever an Empress so wronged and humiliated?

Heigh-ho!

DOCUMENT XII

Fourth Extract from the Journal of Ian Chesterton

My premonition of impending doom has proved to be correct! The galley foundered when almost in sight of Ostia! Strange how often these inexplicably instinctive feelings come from nowhere to warn us, when it's far too late to do anything at all about them. Science cannot explain the phenomenon; and neither can I, not being sufficiently interested perhaps.

At all events, no sooner had a bolt from the black flattened the main-mast – which, happily, collapsed on the galley-master, spattering his odious remains impartially about the bilges – than a rain of splintered spars from above, and a lancing of fanged rocks from below pierced the already straining and complaining hull in so many water-spouting places that some sixth sense told me we were about to sink!

Which we forthwith did; to the accompaniment of the sighs of the dying and the whingeing of the injured.

Then how, you may ask, have I survived to continue my action-packed narrative? Well, Headmaster, if you have been paying attention, you will perhaps remember that my last entry in this journal told of the giant Greek, Delos; whose interminable and vainglorious tales of his prowess in the field of amateur athletics have subsequently abominably bored me? I mean, if it hasn't been flogging, keel-hauling, or short rations, it's been 'Did I ever tell you about the time I won the . . . ' whatever it was! No, simply not on, that sort of thing, in my opinion. However, as the ship disintegrated about our very ears, this loutish loud-mouth was inspired to whisper into one of them that now was our chance!

I looked at him blankly – rather in the manner of Jack Benny regarding Rochester – the 'slow burn', I think it's called – for try as I might, I could detect no chance at all of any outcome to our present predicament other than dismemberment in the wretched wreckage, or drowning in the foul and furious foam. If asked to express a preference, I would probably have opted for the latter, and I said as much. But really, I told him, the matter was of little consequence; and my only serious concern was that, whatever the cause of death, I trusted that the Fates would find it convenient to expedite the business, as there seemed no further point in hanging around.

At this he asked me if I would mind standing up for a moment; and on my complying, somewhat grumpily I fear, with his request, he gripped our rowing bench in his spatulate hands, and wrenching it from its protesting sockets, sprang sideways through a convenient newly-opened hole in the woodwork, muttering sepulchrally 'Follow me!'

I could do little else, being chained to this particular ship's timber by every limb; and presently found myself floundering in his wake as he ploughed through the fish-infested elements towards the dimly visible, far distant, surf-encrusted coast-line in what I took to be a gentleman's freestyle breast-stroke.

I mention fish, because in next to no time I was bitten painfully by a marauding specimen of the filthy brutes – a mackerel, possibly, or a hake, but I have little knowledge of icthyology – at which, I fear, I fainted; although mercifully maintaining buoyancy by virtue of the afore-mentioned thwart.

So, once again, I knew no more; until, this time, I found myself lying on a beach, half smothered in sand and seaweed, the claws of a lobster or some such crustacean protruding from a hole in my toga, while my moronic rescuer snapped the links of our fetters between his terrifying teeth! Or so I supposed in my semi-conscious condition – but it does appear, Headmaster, that metal-bending *was* one of his optional subsidiary subjects in the Pentathlon.

He then suggested that we should head north; pointing out that in the event of recapture, the statutory penalty for escape from a galley was – you've guessed it, Headmaster – death. As, I would like to know, what other penalties *are* there, in this God-forsaken country?

But I am made of heavier mental mettle than he; and have insisted that, no matter what the consequences, we hold our course for Rome – where I pray that I may yet be in time to rescue your history mistress from whatever awaits her in that renownedly degenerate city.

I would also, as you can imagine, like a word or two with the Doctor, whose inane eccentricities have heaped these inconveniences upon us.

I remain – or at least such bits of me do as have been neglected by the Denizens of the Deep – your vilely abused,

         Ian Chesterton, B.Sc.

DOCUMENT XIII

First Selection of Jottings from Nero's Scrapbook

An Ode to Barbara

Fair Barbara! When with fluent pen
I write a poem once again
In praise of Barbara,   *(Good!)*
I wish her trisyllabic name
Were Doris, Ann, Irene, or Jane
Or even Martha,   *(?)*
So that my lost
And tempest-tossed   *(Excellent!!!)*
Unhappy Muse could flout the frost
And storm and form of
      (What? There must be a word . . . Anapaest?
                Perhaps . . . must look it up)
And enter harbour   *(Oh, the tyranny of rhyme!)*
As though embalmed within my arms
Like pigeons perched in potted palms   *(Where?)*
Upon the Costa Brava!   *(Of course!!!)*

Not bad! No, not bad at all, really! I bet Ovid couldn't

have written that! All a question of imagery really. Damn! Wait – I am not entirely sure whether the Costa Brava is part of my Empire at the moment. Bother! If it isn't I shall have to send some general or other to capture it at once, as I do not intend to alter a rhyme so perfectly suited to the delicacy of the sentiments I wish to express; nor, of course, could I ever tolerate the bestowing of such immortality upon a location *not* under my Imperial aegis.

(*Note for future reference:* 'Aegis' would rhyme well with 'Bognor Regis', but I cannot remember if I have invaded Britain recently. I must look at the coloured map on the bathroom wall. If not, then perhaps 'sieges' would serve as an alternative; or is it too obvious?)

Oh, but how can I be expected to remember *anything*, when I am in the grip of such an ecstatic passion as that which inflames my bosom at the time of writing?

(*Is* it passion, or have I been poisoned again by some ill-wisher? The symptoms of love and arsenic are in many respects identical, and never susceptible of easy analysis. The loss of appetite, the dull coat, and the palpitations. The general listlessness . . . yes, I must consult my toxicologist, Locusta, when I've got a moment. She is sure to know; and with her for a friend one hardly needs an enema. Good joke that! Must try it on Juvenal at my forthcoming symposium of the Arts – and if he doesn't laugh, the fellow's for it! Ask him how his Juvenilia's coming along – he hates that!)

But returning to the inflammation of the pectoral region (see above), I am reasonably sure that it *must* be love this time; for seldom in a life devoted to the gratification of my base desires and unbridled lusts have I met so sensual-seeming a seductress as the slave-girl, Barbara. And what is more, I dare to hope that the feeling is mutual; for why otherwise should she have greeted my first attempt to embrace her with such a provocative scream? Or indeed, crowned me with a tea-tray, the fiery-tempered little rogue?

Oh, how I admire a woman of spirit! It makes their eventual conquest so much more agreeable, and their subsequent death so satisfactory all round.

In fact, that is what first attracted me to my present wife, Poppea – although so long ago that it now seems unreal. Must be all of twelve months, I suppose, since I first resolved to make her mine. She had a certain shark-infested beauty in those days, and I used to call her 'Poppy'. Well, I still do, of course, but not with much enthusiasm. No, she seems to have gone soft, and devotes herself entirely to good works. She's always ready to put up a Praetorian guard who's forgotten the curfew. In fact, I have even known her to visit the barracks at all hours of the night, just to see if there might be any young recruit feeling the cold.

This sort of thing is getting her a good, albeit, short-name; and it must stop before my own authority is undermined. She is becoming altogether too popular with the men, and if I cannot depend on their loyalty I am lost; because for some reason nobody seems to like me much . . .

Later: I was right – I can depend on no one! Tigillinius, the deaf-mute slave I keep around for laughs, has just informed me in his impeccable sign-language that the Corinthian musician, Maximus Petullian, craves an audience of me! How can this be (and why, incidentally, can't he attract an audience of his own?) when only yesterday I despatched my most trusted centurion and the assassin Ascaris, of whom he spoke so highly, to make an end of the fellow? Have I been betrayed, or are they simply inefficient?

Well, I suppose I shall have to see the man if he *is* still alive, or my reputation as a patron of the Arts will surely suffer. But this meeting is one I have been anxious to avoid, as I detest being bearded in my lion's den (now, there's a happy thought!) by the competition.

Oh, the loneliness of power . . .

DOCUMENT XIV

Fourth Letter from
Legionary (Second Class) Ascaris

Dear Mum,

The Fates have smiled upon me in my sewer, and about time too, wouldn't you say? Towards dusk I emerged briefly for a breath or two, and was about to sink my scruples once more, when who should I see but my recent victim and late assailant, the apparently indestructible Maximus Petullian! He appeared to be lecturing some bit of a girl on the architectural heritage in which we all take a pride; and as he seemed to be off his guard for once, I resolved to follow him with the stealth for which I am a catch-phrase, and was in time to see him enter your actual palace, bold as you please!

Well, he is going to regret that, I can tell you; for just as soon as I can purchase another dagger, I shall be about his person with it, and so redeem my fallen fortunes.

There being a queue at the armourers, I take this opportunity of letting you know my intentions, and remain

Your resourceful boy,

Ascaris.

PS. Why do you never reply to my letters? Have I offended you in some way?

DOCUMENT XV

Fifth Extract from the Doctor's Diary

A curious incident!

On presenting ourselves at Nero's palace, Vicki and I were not at first able to attract any attention; but after some time spent in examining the plunder of Gloria Mundi, with which the entrance hall was crammed to such an extent as to make movement difficult, I inadvertently knocked over a status of Venus, thereby severing both its arms; and I was then at once approached by a court official who looked at me enquiringly.

I introduced myself as Maximus Petullian, and stated my business – not an easy matter under the circumstances. But my speech had been well rehearsed in anticipation of the occasion; and after some five minutes I fancied I had covered most of the relevant facts material to my purpose, namely an interview with the Emperor, who, I had reason to believe, was expecting me.

The official no longer looked enquiring, but merely blank; and having done so, pointed in turn to his ears and his mouth. I looked at them closely, but found nothing at all remarkable to justify the gesture; until Vicki suggested that the man might be deaf and dumb. This ridiculous theory proved to be correct, and meant that I had wasted a good deal of valuable time; but fortunately I am well acquainted with the rudiments of sign language, and so was able to repeat my introductory remarks in mime.

At this he nodded with complete understanding, and indicated that we should take our seats on a singularly uncomfortable marble bench, fashioned in the shape of two obese babies – Romulus and Remus, presumably – being suckled by an irritable looking she-wolf, while he went to inform his master of our presence.

It was while we were thus engaged that we were approached by the very centurion who only that morning had bilked me of the price of bed and board; and I was rebuking the fellow roundly, when he laughed in an unpleasant manner, grabbed me by the lapels of my toga, and hauled me to my feet, breathing garlic in my face, and making no offer of restitution.

Now, as is well known, I am not to be trifled with in such a way, and I instantly gave him a push of such force as to precipitate him backwards on to the seat I had just vacated.

And now occurred the curious incident of which I wrote at the beginning of this entry: I was rolling up my sleeves in case of further fisticuffs when, through the tapestry behind the bench there emerged an arm holding a dagger, which it buried to the hilt between the centurion's shoulder-blades, or scapuli!

As usual, Vicki screamed – and I do wish she wouldn't, as it tends to attract unwelcome attention. However, as the man fell forwards onto his unpleasantly contorted face, I at once drew aside the curtain; and to my astonishment revealed the bestial form of the assassin Ascaris – he who had so ineffectively assaulted me in my bedroom the previous evening!

For a moment he stood there, looking at the fallen form of his officer with what I can only describe as horror and dawning remorse; and then with a loud cry of 'Oh, my cripes! That's torn it, that has!' he left the premises by the main entrance at a stumbling run, and disappeared into the gathering darkness.

I felt it prudent not to follow, having already had occasion to observe of what villainy he tries so hard to be capable; and was in the process of concealing the body, when a firm hand descended on my shoulder – but rather to my surprise in a congratulatory rather than an accusative manner – and a hoarse voice whispered 'Well done, Max!'

I turned to encounter the unsavoury gaze of the toad, Tavius, who had last been observed purchasing the slave-girl who resembled Barbara, some hours previously. He wasted no further time in civilities, but helped me, winking and chuckling horribly the while, to rearrange the arras over the bleeding remains; and this having been completed to his satisfaction, he informed me sepulchrally that the Emperor would see me now.

Regretfully I decided that Vicki should not

accompany me to the presence, at least on this occasion, as she was still sobbing and shuddering convulsively in a way which might well have created a bad impression at a first meeting. So, instructing her to avail herself of this unrivalled opportunity to explore a palace not normally open to the public, and to meet me by the corpse in an hour's time, I followed my strangely repulsive partner in crime to the Imperial quarters for my first momentous interview – more of which anon.

For the moment I will only add that I begin to suspect I may have become unwittingly involved in some kind of conspiracy – and the thought is not an easy one to live with. It is my most firmly held contention – which I am constantly repeating to Vicki and the others – that we must under no circumstances ever allow ourselves to be placed in such a situation that we inadvertently alter the course of History! No, our visit to Rome must be purely an educational vacation.

Well, we shall have to see what further transpires, and modify our behaviour accordingly . . .

DOCUMENT XVI

Fifth Extract from the Journal of Ian Chesterton

I fear I may have annoyed my enormous companion, Delos, but really there is little I can do to appease the man at the moment. But appease him somehow I must, since he is shortly to be my opponent in a gladiatorial contest; and even were he to enter the arena in a good-humoured and sporting spirit, he would still make a formidable adversary – witness the snapping of chains, and the wrenching of benches – and I do not care to think of what he might be capable were he to be in a really bad temper!

For the last twenty-four hours, however, he has refused to respond to my friendly overtures, and merely sits in a corner of the dungeon where we are detained, muttering and glowering.

Am I going too fast for you, Headmaster? Then perhaps I should explain the concatenation of unforseen circumstances which have brought us to this pretty pass; and you will then understand, I hope, why my normally high spirits are in abeyance at the moment.

You will remember that after my rescue from

shipwreck, I overbore the, what seemed to me, rather craven arguments by which Delos urged me to accompany him in a northerly direction, there to go into hiding until our death by drowning should be assumed by the authorities? But not for me the life of the fugitive! And I insisted, *perhaps* unwisely as it now appears, that instead we should head directly for Rome, where I intended to strain every sinew not already ruptured by my recent experiences, in a search for my unfortunate colleague, Barbara Wright. And in spite of the outcome, I *still* maintain that under the then circumstances this was the correct and honourable course of action, and that morally speaking I could have adopted no other, as I'm sure you will agree.

However, on arriving at the gates of the Eternal City – or is that Jerusalem, I can never remember – the ill-fortune which, since my first meeting with the Doctor, has followed at my heels like an unwanted timber-wolf, once more took over the control of my affairs, and quickly slipped me the staccato tomato – if you will forgive the somewhat mixed metaphor.

Urging Delos to look as inconspicuous as possible for a man some eight feet tall and broad with it, I at once began to pursue my enquiries, casually asking the passers-by if they happened to have encountered a pleasant-looking girl with a British accent, who when last seen was wearing a sort of crimson and gold toga with matching accessories.

In spite of my companion's misgivings, I was myself quite satisfied that this course of action, pursued methodically and patiently, would eventually produce results; and indeed it did, although not the ones I had innocently anticipated. For amongst the very first of the persons I accosted in this manner was the slave-trader, Sevcheria; who informed me that by a curious coincidence he had sold someone answering to that description for a record price only yesterday; and that she was, to the best of his knowledge, not only more or less alive and moderately well, but living in jeopardy as personal hand-maiden to the Empress Poppea.

But what, might he make so bold as to ask, was *I* doing, so far away from the hellish hulk where he had confidently expected me to spend the rest of my natural, groaning under the lash, and occupied in the carrying far and near of fur and myrrh, and furthermore of apes and peacocks, which had always seemed to him to be remarkably unmarketable, and rather surprising? Never mind, however, for the question was clearly academic – at which he laughed. Why, I wonder? – and I really needn't bother to reply at the moment, because I would presently be needing my breath for other matters of a more violent nature. He then summoned a passing platoon of Praetorians, informed them that Delos and I were two escaped galley-slaves, and asked if they didn't think they ought to do something about it?

Early in the ensuing mêlée, I was perhaps fortunately knocked unconscious again. Delos, however, having apparently broken the arms, legs, and necks of several of our assailants, sustained several severe cuts and contusions; which he is now nursing whilst growling to himself and glaring at me. But I really do not see how I could have acted otherwise, and I have told him as much. To little effect, however . . .

As to our forthcoming gladiatorial contest . . . Well, being, I confess, slightly surprised to find myself still alive, I asked the reason for this unexpected clemency of the guard who brought our breakfast. It seems that Delos has been recognised as a former athlete and very heavyweight contender (Really! And after I had made a particular point of asking him to remain incognito!); and apparently one of Nero's favourite diversions is to watch two friends beat each other to a pulp in the arena – winner to go free. I assume that this latter provision is to ensure that they both give of their best, and pull no punches!

I hastened to point out that Delos and I were no longer particularly friendly for some reason; and since this might take the gilt off the gingerbread as far as Nero was concerned, wouldn't it be better to dream up an alternative programme?

He informed me that the only one he could think of which might find favour, would involve augmenting the cast with a pack – or pride – of lions; which, if I cared to glance through the window, I would note were kept in constant readiness for such an entertainment. Perhaps I would then care to state a preference, and he would be pleased to convey my feelings in the matter to the Emperor – although, of course, he could promise nothing, it all depending on what sort of mood His Nibs was in . . .

I had already noted that whereas some of the lions were asleep and appeared amiable enough, there were one or two which were manifestly of a more irritable disposition, and gnawing on dry bones in angry anticipation of feeding time. I was, therefore, about to reject this alternative, when my attention was caught by Delos doing his press-ups, and now I am not so sure!

I must obviously give the matter my earnest consideration in the few hours remaining to me; and meanwhile remain your always optimistic, but probably doomed 'Stinks Tutor'!

                                          Ian Chesterton

DOCUMENT XVII

Second Extract from the Commonplace Book of Poppea Sabina

An air of intrigue broods over this damn' palace like a pall, and I find it increasingly difficult to get on with the housework. Even to bring this little note-book up to date requires more time than I can really spare from keeping my wits about me, and ensuring that I am not imposed upon or murdered in some way. But it must, of course, be done; or future generations will never know the most secret thoughts and private fears of a very young Empress, who is only trying to meet her responsibilities under increasingly difficult and vexing circumstances. Heigh-ho!

Today, for instance, I was on my way to meet just one of these responsibilities – a centurion in whom I have been taking a semi-professional interest – when I noticed that the statue of Venus in the foyer had been damaged, probably beyond repair, by the loss of both its arms! A girl with less reason to be suspicious might have attributed the damage to the carelessness of a house-maid while dusting; but the matter is not to be so simply explained. No, it has often been remarked by my admirers that the sculpture bears a striking resemblance to me; which not only accounts for its value, but makes me tremble to suspect the damage is a barely concealed threat of violence pending to my person.

I therefore reeled against the wall in an agony of apprehension, as one does at such times; and while thus engaged was horrified to feel beneath my little hands, as they fluttered about and clutched at the priceless tapestries, the well-known outline of a human form!

Dragging aside the draperies, with what intimations of mortality I leave you, gentle reader, to imagine, I discovered the bleeding body of the very centurion to whom I had promised half an hour before dinner; and surely these two closely associated mishaps cannot be mere coincidence?

This brutal and abrupt cancellation of my assignation left me, as you can imagine, not only all of a tremble but in a temper too, for I had not as yet quite finished with the wretched man; and it was therefore in a mood of some tantrum and termagence that I hurried at once to the chamber of Locusta, the palace poisoner, whose services have so often been of some assistance to me. For if, as I could only be almost certain, my husband were behind these twin outrages, then it was my intention to show him that two could play at that game, by instantly securing the destruction of Barbara, the new slave-girl he fancies he fancies – and let that be a lesson to him!

Locusta was busy about her cauldron as usual; and

although she received me politely enough – as what else *could* she do, I would like to know, my being Empress and all? – I thought I detected an evasive strain in her cracked and quavering tones as she told me that just now she was up to here in orders!

'Oh, and from whom?' I demanded, as imperiously as my *distraite* condition would allow.

'Why, dearie,' she told me, 'from your lovely husband, of course. You know he's got this banquet on tomorrow, and he likes to be ready for anything; as is surely only natural, what with all these conspiracies we've been having lately. Can't be too careful, that's what I always say.'

I told her, somewhat stiffly, that I was not in the least interested in what she always said; and added that she would attend to my requirements at once, if she knew what was good for her!

At this she cackled in an unpleasant manner, and informed me that it was knowing what was *bad* for people which had made her the woman she was today.

I summoned a sickly smile from somewhere, not wishing to offend the old hag unduly; whereupon she softened somewhat, and said she'd do what she could to fit me in.

'Who's the lucky victim to be, then?' she enquired. 'Anyone you know, or is it just a game of "Swap the Goblet" again?'

By a curious coincidence, it was at this moment that Barbara herself ran rapidly along the corridor, clanking with unsolicited gifts obviously given to her by my husband; since he presently appeared in lolloping pursuit, yet another golden bracelet clutched in his flaccid hands – an item which I at once recognised as being his anniversary present to me!

Overcome with mortification, the shame of my betrayal, and a certain amount of ungovernable fury, I fear I so far forgot myself as to hiss like a snake, and to spit in the general direction of their retreating figures; and Locusta took the point at once.

'So that's the little lady, is it?' she asked, as I nodded speechlessly between expectorations.

'Well, there's nothing too nasty, in my opinion, for the sort of sly-boots who uses the well-known wiles of the seraglio to come between an Emperor and his missus. Leave it to me, dearie. It'll be my pleasure to mix her something really special in the way of lethal overdoses . . .'

And she pottered off to her potion pantry.

Can I trust her? And indeed, can I trust anyone? It is sometimes difficult for a comparatively inexperienced girl to know which way to turn.

Heigh-ho, once more!

DOCUMENT XVIII

A Poisoner Remembers (Extract from The Autobiography of Locusta)

It was another busy day in the pharmaceutical department, and I remember reflecting that if business continued to improve at that rate, it would kill itself off before it got fairly started. And where would I be then, I asked myself, having only one pair of hands at that stage in my career, and that couple time-worn and gnarled with arthritis or some such affliction; which in the present state of medical knowledge we do not truly understand, although I work constantly at a wonder drug in my spare time, if any, keeping a sharp lookout for unwanted side-effects, because who knows when they might not come in useful?

No, what I really needed, it seemed to me, if I was to give of my worst whenever requested, was an assistant to take the weight off my crucibles now and then, so as to let me get on with a spot of high level government research into astrology like the rest of my coven, who were doing very well for themselves, thank you, with horoscopes of the famous, while I slaved away for peanuts in my rotten grotto!

No sooner had this long but half-formulated thought been

caught in my attention than there came a knock on the laboratory door, causing me to drop a hot goblet on my frock and emit an eldrich scream, and there stood a pert young party who asked me if I could direct her to the Imperial Apartments as she seemed to have got lost.

'A likely tale!' I thought, and was about to invite her to a final wine-tasting, when it occurred to me that here might be just the apprentice my enterprises required, and I asked her if she had ever considered a career in toxicology, as it was a growth industry right now?

She said she'd try anything once, and introduced herself as Vicki, of no fixed address, which could be convenient, I thought, if the arrangement didn't work out. So I agreed to give her an hour or so's probationary period, during which she could make herself generally useful taking the drudgery out of my work by handling the victim-to-crypt delivery side of the business.

And since she was on her way to the throne room any old how, perhaps as a favour to the Empress she wouldn't mind taking up a couple of sparkling drinks – *this* one for Nero, and *that* one for his new lady friend who was almost certain to be with him round about now, and if not then give it to whoever was, as it seemed a pity to waste it.

I then turned my back for a moment, and was gratified to see in the mirror that she immediately switched the glasses, which I had depended upon, having misinformed her as to which was which.

So here I had a thoroughly dishonest and unscrupulous child who was almost certain to give every satisfaction and sudden death quite impartially.

It seemed I had chosen well . . .

DOCUMENT XIX

Letter from Barbara Wright

Nero, enough!

What is the use of going on like this? I am not unaware of your interest in me, having received from your clammy hands to date more priceless jewels of the Orient than I can possibly wear without appearing to be vulgar.

And while we are on the subject, can you really believe that if I were to incorporate Cleopatra's coronet into my coiffure, such ostentation would not arouse your wife's criticism, should she notice the adornment?

I do not wish to hurt your feelings by sending back these items; but under separate cover you will find your no doubt well meant oysters, which I am returning unopened, being conscious of their reputedly aphrodisiacal properties.

I would have preferred not to have to write this somewhat cruel letter, hoping to have eliminated the necessity for it by my previous behaviour; which has included, you may recall, striking you with a metal tea-tray at our first meeting, and subsequently screaming at your passionate approach, shuddering at your tentative touch, et cetera.

But since, apparently, you are incapable of taking a hint, there are certain things which *must* be said if our already unpleasant relationship is not to degenerate further – although to what loathsome depths it is susceptible of descending, I prefer not to think!

You should, therefore, know – in all fairness – that it is useless for you to attempt to conceal your unsavoury self beneath the simulacrum of a sugar-satyr; since, as a sometime teacher of history, I am fully cognizant of that suppurating septicaemia of the so-called soul which invests your festering facade with the dropsical dross of all possible nostrils!

Let us be honest: I do not find you in the least bit attractive.

I am sorry if this seems harsh, but I hope that you will feel able to forgive me in time, and allow me to remain your unmolested, but in other respects, obedient servant,

M/S Barbara Wright.

DOCUMENT XX

Second Selection of Jottings from Nero's Scrapbook

She loves me! I feel almost sure she does! Why else should she have written me a letter concealing her true feelings – which must be almost uncontrollable to have driven her to adopt such a course? And, having adopted it, the poor besotted child has rendered it vain by signing herself M/S – which can, I think, only be intended as an abbreviation of Mus!

Well, my little Mouse – if that is what you wish me to call you – I shall be your great big pussy cat, just see if I'm not!

Further to which, as I was awaiting – why should *I* have to wait? It's too bad! – the arrival of the itinerant ballad-monger, Maximus Petullian, I was very naturally musing on lions and their maintenance; and the thought occurred to me that perhaps I have inadvertently been cruel – well, just a *tiny* bit – to use them as I do. Because all this time I have been feeding them with Christians by the arena-full, and have never once thought to ask myself if this was an adequate diet.

One imagines the King of Beasts turning to his lady,

and grumbling, 'Christians *again*? Why can't you ever stay in and *cook* something?'

And I see his point – I really do! It must be dreadfully monotonous for them, and I accept the criticism. Very well then; in future they shall have *roast* Christian! I see an avenue of blazing human torches, down which the great cats pad, selecting the joint they prefer at will, and feeling, I am sure, the better for it. Their condition is bound to improve in no time, and they will fawn upon their benefactor in the most gratifying manner. I cannot imagine why I have never thought of this before, and I blame myself for my lack of consideration.

(Memo: Ask Max. P. if Christian.)

I had reached this point in my reflections when the adorable Barbara entered the room, saw me, blanched provocatively, squeaked enticingly, and went out again.

I at once forgot all but my, by now, routine pursuit of the beautiful houri; and, snatching up some golden gew-gaw from my wife's dressing table, I chased her lithely about the endless corridors of my palatial love-nest, along which she fled me like some shy gazelle; and I am reasonably confident that she would have allowed me to catch her on this occasion, had not my winged feet encountered a loose, leopard-skin draught-stopper, which brought my subtle courtship to a premature and undignified close, and left me spread-eagled on the floor of the very room from which I had started out with such high hopes!

I remarked, 'Whoops!', or some such expletive; and

rose laboriously to my feet before the astonished gaze of my musical rival, Maximus Petullian, whose impending visit I fear I had quite forgotten in my excitement.

Hardly the entrance I would have chosen; nor would it have been my wish to find the soporific Poppy amongst those present! For, as I have confided in these pages previously, if a marriage is going to last, it will never be my fault. I have, in fact, already written her obituary, and cannot wait to publish. But for the moment she is still Empress, I suppose, and must be accorded as scant and grudging respect as I can contrive; at any rate, in public.

So I waved her graciously to a foot-stool, and taking my place on the malachite and carbuncle encrusted catafalque I keep for emergencies, I asked my visitor his business.

I had intended the question to be rhetorical, at most, as I had not the slightest interest in learning the answer; but to my utter annoyance, he at once produced a sheaf of closely written documents, and informed me that he had taken the liberty of preparing an agenda for this, and possibly subsequent meetings, should we not have time to cover every point he wished to raise during the course of this one evening.

I explained, with as much self-control as I could muster on the spur of the moment, that I was a very busy Emperor – at which Poppy laughed nastily – and that he should consider himself damn' lucky to have the privilege of seeing me at all, never mind any nonsense about on-going and open-ended discussions, thank you!

In fact, the only reason he was here, as far as I was concerned, was so that he could give me a tune – preferably short – on the box, there; which would give me an opportunity of judging whether he met the high standard necessary to participate in the 'Nero Caesar in Concert' concert, billed for the banquet tomorrow.

I was pleased to see that he faltered slightly on hearing this; but rapidly, confound him, recovering his impertinent composure, he declared that there would be plenty of time for all that sort of nonsense later; but first he was anxious to hear my proposals for the relieving of traffic congestion on the Appian Way, the amelioration of slum conditions in the inner city areas, and for the gradual phasing out of slavery in favour of the principle of 'one man, one vote', so popular during the Republic! Oh yes, and one other thing: why did people keep trying to kill him?

Well, on the evidence available, I could have answered his last question then and there – a justifiable homicide it would be, if ever there was one; but being anxious to preserve the reputation for Sweet Reason which I have to insist on, I contented myself with saying that there was a lot of assassination about just now, so he mustn't think he was being discriminated against unfairly. As to the Appian Way, I had already decided to abolish pedestrians in order to facilitate free-flow; the slums were certainly a burning problem (here I smiled slightly and secretly) which was receiving my most pernicious pyromania (Here I smiled broadly and publicly, to show that I didn't mean it really); and, finally, I said that I didn't see what he had against slavery, as personally I was very fond of slaves – at which Poppy again laughed nastily – and, in any case, I couldn't do everything at once now, could I? There was my poetry to get on with for instance, not to mention my musical compositions for augmented strings – and by the way, speaking of which, what about his obliging with an arpeggio or two, as requested? (One has to be firm on these occasions, hasn't one, or people take advantage?)

Not, of course, that I really *wanted* to listen to the fellow play; but nevertheless I arranged myself amongst the cushions of the catafalque in an attitude of artistic receptivity; closing my eyes, as I have seen critics do when listening to my own performances. Although exactly why one is supposed to hear better with the eyes shut, I have never properly understood.

However, I soon opened them again, for seldom in a life devoted to aesthetics and their capture have my ears been assaulted by such a frantic cacophony as presently shattered a crystal candelabrum of which I had been particularly fond.

'Pardon me, Petullian,' I said, interrupting his frenetic threnody before it cracked the plaster, 'but as a matter of courtesy, might it not have been better to have *tuned* your malodoron, or whatever it is, before entering these premises? I have no wish to discourage a fellow practitioner, but I warn you that if you ever do anything like that again, I must seriously consider having you dropped in the Bosphorus!'

He regarded me in a pained manner.

'You didn't like it?' he enquired; needlessly, I'd have thought. 'Well, of course, that was only the introductory exposition. I develop the main theme later . . .'

'Not in this palace, you don't!' I told him.

'I appreciate that to your untutored ears . . .'

'Leave my ears out of it!'

'All I'm trying to say is that I have developed a wholly new technique . . .'

'I advise you to forget it at once!'

He sighed deeply. 'You can't halt progress, you know . . .' he ventured unwisely.

'Who can't?' I snarled.

'I mean, you can't uninvent something, once it's there. And what I've invented is the ultratonic scale.'

'A what and tonic?'

'It's a totally new theory of harmonics. I thought it would interest an enlightened despot like your goodself . . . ?'

'You were wrong! It sets my teeth sideways, if you must know . . .'

'You will find,' he continued complacently, 'that before very long – speaking cosmically, that is – it will have completely superseded the outworn Classical and Romantic traditions, which are merely the symbols of a reactionary preoccupation with jolly good tunes.'

The man was manifestly mad; and I was about to strike him with a suggestion, when I suddenly thought of a better one . . .

'Look, I don't want to be unfair,' I told him; 'so why don't you give the complete piece an airing at the Nero

Fest tomorrow? Then we'll be able to see how it goes down in front of a packed house, eh? And if I'm wrong, I'll apologise – the way I always do!'

He looked apprehensive, as well he might: because if I'm any judge, no self-respecting mob of promenaders is going to stand for that sort of thing for long without eviscerating, or otherwise incommoding, the performer. Which would save my recently rather overworked lions the trouble.

'I'm not entirely sure that the world is ready . . .' he began.

'Well, there's only one way to find out, isn't there?' I comforted him. 'Good – so that's settled, then. Oh, by the way, I'd better have the title for the programme notes, hadn't I?'

He swallowed something, blushed, and then, 'Thermodynamic Functions,' he mumbled modestly.

It is perhaps fortunate that, at this moment, a girl came in with some drinks . . .

DOCUMENT XXI

Sixth Extract from the Journal of Ian Chesterton

Well, the die is cast – but whether for ill or good only Time, as they say, will tell; and there doesn't seem to be a lot of that left, from where I'm standing! Or slumping, rather, for I have been chained to the cell wall in such a manner as to prevent my either standing or sitting comfortably; and if that is a recommended discipline for the night previous to a title bout, I'm surprised, to say the least!

In fact, it is only by the most painful contortions that I am able to continue this chronicle at all, but I am determined not to relapse into apathy; and it is only the thought that, somewhere in the far distant future, I have a friend – for so I consider you, Headmaster – which sustains me through this dark vigil.

You will have gathered from my reference to tomorrow's contest that I have opted for single combat – to the death! – with Delos; rather than to go rushing round the ring with a lot of strange lions of uncertain temper, and I can only hope I have chosen wisely.

The weapon I have selected is the javelin – perhaps you may remember my prowess on the dart-board at the staff social? – and my defence is to be a weighted net, with which I shall hope to entangle my vast opponent's sword arm at the first opportunity; thereby rendering him powerless, and at my mercy. Which mercy I shall, of course, be prepared to grant. For I recall a film featuring Kirk Douglas, in a role similar to my own – *Spartacus*, I think – when the two combatants spared each other's lives, and then together turned on their tormenters with some degree of success.

I put this suggestion to Delos, but he merely regarded me pityingly; and the only concession he seemed prepared to make, was that he would do it quick, when the time came, as he was anxious to get back to his home in Greece, and not hang about.

He then summoned our gaoler, and arranged to be given separate accommodation for the night, as he wanted to get a good night's sleep before starting; a thing he would find impossible if I was going to keep on making fatuous suggestions every five minutes.

For my part, I was quite relieved to see him go, since he does not so much snore as snarl and eructate alternately; and I can only hope that the morning will find him in a more amenable mood. For I still maintain that, back to back, against whatever odds, we might well hold off our adversaries for long enough to make good our escape.

But will the dawn never come? And if it does, as seems likely, then what will it bring? These and a hundred other rhetorical questions flood my brain; but no time for more now, as I must get a spot of shut-eye myself, if I'm to be anything like on top form.

Your very sincere, but often apprehensive,

Ian Chesterton

DOCUMENT XXII

Third Extract from the Commonplace Book of Poppea Sabina

I am more than ever convinced that unsteady is the head which sports a crown, or some such; and it is quite right to be so under the circumstances. Which are that my unsought consort will shortly qualify for the laughing academy if he carries on like this!

Today when I visited our cosy old throne-room, expecting – not unreasonably, I think – to catch him at it with the demon Barbara, I found instead *another* nutcase (What *is* it about the lyre which does this to people?) who proceeded to lecture me on the hydrostatic principles of the aqueduct, if I understood him correctly.

I was backing away to summon assistance on the alarm gong, when my husband entered – on his stomach, for some reason – and immediately engaged the man in a totally incomprehensible conversation, bearing, I think, on aspects of political economy; culminating in a lyre obligato of such dissonance as to set me swooning, swan-like in a dream of sudden screams in saw-mills.

I was roused from this temporary inverted coma by the entrance of yet another new slave-girl, bearing two drinks on a tray; at one of which I clutched, in an unusually palsied paroxysm of the dipsomania which has troubled me from infancy, when I was given pause by her murmuring as she curtsied, 'From the lady Locusta, ma'am;' upon hearing which I shrank back from the proffered cordial as a cobra does from a mongoose, and offered it to my husband, saying, 'Nero, my god, to thee!' or some similar spontaneous quip.

However, he had already raised the other glass half-way to his unpleasant lips, when our visitor, the gnomic musician, addressed the serving wench as 'Vicki', followed by an exclamation mark.

'*Veni, vidi, vici!*' she agreed, with a saucy wink, before he could continue, but too late to dispel the impression that they had somewhere met before; and Nero, who is sometimes as quick on the uptake as the only slightly insane, lowered his own goblet thoughtfully, saying that for some reason he no longer felt thirsty, and perhaps I would like it? An offer I declined with an amused sneer.

Whereupon, having been through this 'Pass the Poisoned Chalice' routine together so often on long winter evenings, we both extended our toxic what's-its in the general direction of Mad Max and his young confederate; who confirmed our dawning suspicions by rejecting the blue and bubbling beverages, the former accompanying his refusal with a lecture on the evils of strong drink, which was overdoing things rather, I thought, unless he really *did* know what was in it!

So, as usual, we put the matter to the test by summoning an independent arbitrator, the wretched Tigillinius drawing the short straw on this occasion; who shortly thereafter expired in a cloud of steam, and with what I'm sure would have been a strangled scream on his lips, had the poor fellow ever been capable of speech.

Although shocked by the occurrence, Max was clearly mollified to some extent by this immediate justification of his temperance principles, and later the conversation became general, as far as I remember. It was soon revealed that the suspect serving wench was, in fact, Petullian's ward, who had only been helping Locusta out below stairs to fill in the time, so all misunderstandings were resolved – or as nearly so as they *ever* are in this abode of love and trust: and we invited them to join us in watching a gladiatorial contest featuring two recaptured galley-slaves tomorrow morning.

This invitation the old man rather churlishly refused, however, on the grounds that Vicki was far too young to watch so bloodthirsty a spectacle, however educational it might be, since it was likely also to deprave and corrupt (and where's the harm in that, *I* would like to know?); while he himself felt that his time would be better spent in rehearsing his piece for its premiere in the evening, the poor fool!

So with many false expressions of mutual goodwill we parted; and I now look forward to seeing them torn to pieces by a howling mob of brutal and licentious music lovers after the performance.

Just another boring day in the life of a very ordinary Roman Empress. Heigh-ho as usual.

And so to bed.

DOCUMENT XXIII

Fifth Letter from Legionary (Second Class) Ascaris

Dear Mum,

I have already let you know the dodgy outcome of my last vain attempt to redeem 'my fallen fortunes', which ended in the sad death of my commanding officer, but was an accident, as he would be the first to admit was he so able. But without his valuable testimony as to his sitting in the wrong seat at the time of the stabbing, I have thought it best to keep my low profile in the sewer for a bit longer while things blow over me. Which I now believe they may have done, since no word has reached me to the contrary, or indeed at all for some time.

But I cannot rest here easy while Petullian lives, for he and the screaming baggage who must also go both saw me do the job, and so it is now them or me, as I'm sure you will quite understand. So here I go again, with a heart as high as the rest of me, to sort out the pair of them for keeps this time, let us hope!

After which I should be over-ripe for promotion if there is any justice; and a credit to you, like you

suggested I should try being sometime.
Still no letter. Your very puzzled

                                                Ascaris.

DOCUMENT XXIV

Sixth Extract from the Doctor's Diary

Neither of the Neros having had the grace to offer us accommodation for the night, and the events of the evening having persuaded me of the inadvisability of dining with them – what a very *odd* couple, to be sure! – I eventually succeeded in booking two somewhat squalid but quite adequate rooms in one of the city's poorer quarters; and we retired early after an interesting meal of ants' eggs sautéed in some sheep's milk.

Personally I slept well; but in the morning Vicki was in a refractory mood, complaining of bats in her attic and rats in her mattress, and similar irritabilia, until I quite lost patience with her, and suggested she take her breakfast of stewed lampreys back to bed, while I found a quiet corner of the palace to perfect my concert piece.

But today it was difficult to find any sequestered restroom suited to my purpose, since all available space was seething with spectators who had come to watch the big fight; so, skirting the arena and its environs, I eventually came to a balcony overlooking what I presumed to be the zoological gardens, where several fine specimens of *felis leo* were taking a siesta in the shade, and here I determined to rehearse.

I confess to being well pleased with my first attempt at atonal composition, *Thermodynamic Functions*, since to me it typifies the eternal conflict between Art and Audience – which is brought to an altogether alienating crescendo of raucous discords in the final movement.

But it begins relatively quietly, with a wailing lament for lost innocence, modulating freely through a good many keys, until it reaches the long and lachrymose *legato* passage which expounds the violent argument – without, of course, resolving it in the slightest! If you follow me?

And I find it especially satisfactory that I, a scientist, should have so easily been able to achieve what unborn generations of professional concert-goers are bound to find extremely difficult.

So it was with a certain amount of justified complacency that I reached for the first bundle of chords – and struck them with all the strength at my disposal . . .

It has been said, I believe, that music hath charms to soothe the savage breast; but on this occasion at least, I was interested to note that the effect was entirely different.

As my ineffably incredible *arpeggios* sank amongst the hitherto somnolent carnivores before me, they instantly opened indignant eyes, and backed bristling towards the opposite wall of their enclosure, snarling and spitting suspiciously in all directions!

Simultaneously a loud and angry cry from behind me caused me to duck, and, as I did so, over my head flew that squat and unsavoury figure whose frequent attempts on my life have been such an unwelcome feature of my stay in Italy.

Instinctively I struck out at it in passing with my lyre, unfortunately once again entangling the man's flailing arms in the strings; so that as he descended into the lions' den he was carrying the instrument with him; whereupon it emitted one last despairing diapason, and then disintegrated – I would say irreparably, confound the fellow!

The lions, for their part, looked at the cracked apparatus resentfully, then rose to their paws and paced implacably towards my assailant, flexing their biceps in the manner of cats who are going to settle this thing here and now.

Obviously the assassin received the same impression, for he now ran whimpering around the limited space available to him, like a mouse in a bucket, making a series of despairing and ineffectual leaps towards the parapet.

Why I should have helped the man I am not sure, for I certainly owed him no consideration after his previous behaviour towards me; but I had noticed that near to where I was standing there was a winch mechanism from which ropes descended to a sliding door, which I presumed – erroneously, as it transpired – led to the beasts' sleeping quarters. If, I reasoned, I opened this door just sufficiently to allow of his escape, and then instantly lowered it behind him, he would be trapped intact within their dormitory until such time as he could be delivered to the proper authorities, and made to give an account of himself.

So: 'This way, my good fellow; to your immediate left!' I advised him; and, releasing the rachet, seized the handle of the pulley.

Unfortunately, however, I had neglected to observe that the device was fitted with counter-weights, so that I was at once flung from my feet into the air, where I described a large arc; while the door flew open to its full aperture. And, as he sprang through it, closely pursued by the entire, outraged pack – or pride – I realised with sudden dismay that this exit led, not to some inner sanctum, but to the gladiatorial arena; where, as I judged from the swelling cheers of the multitude, the morning's unappealing performance had just started . . .

DOCUMENT XV

Seventh Extract from the Journal of Ian Chesterton

The widely anticipated dawn at last arrived, heralded by my gaoler with the news that it looked like being a good house, as there was queuing at all prices.

I derived what cheer I could from this announcement – for one doesn't, of course, wish one's death to pass entirely unnoticed – and was then led through the damp catacombs, given my weapons, and ushered into the arena; where my appearance was greeted in a manner reminiscent of the Lower Fourth disapproving, as ever, of their examination results.

But I had little time to reflect on the manifest bias of the audience, for my attention was at once drawn to the box of the Emperor Nero himself, where to my astonishment I saw that Barbara Wright made one of the Imperial Party.

I ventured a wave, to which she responded with a barely perceptible flicker of the fingers, my gesture having been intercepted by a lady who could only have been Poppea, and who thereupon blew me a kiss.

Nero glanced irritably at both girls, and declared

that that would be quite enough of that kind of thing, thank you; but any subsequent remarks he may have uttered were drowned by the storm of exaggerated cheering which greeted the entrance of my adversary, the giant Delos.

He appeared to have slept well, and advanced to meet me with hand outstretched; but on my being silly enough to shake it, he crushed nerveless several of my fingers in his iron grip – which is the sort of thing which gets wrestling a bad name, in my opinion. Nevertheless it went down very well with the crowd; and having acknowledged their approval, he said 'For goodness sake, don't make such a fuss, or they'll think it's all faked! Now, pull yourself together: first of all we have to address the Emperor.'

'As what?' I groaned, not being entirely sure of the protocol.

'*Nos morituri te salutamus,*' he suggested; 'it's usual.'

And on my looking rather blank, he kindly translated the remark as: 'We who are about to die salute you.'

'Yes, but look here,' I objected, 'if you'll only listen to me for a moment, I'm sure you'll see that neither of us need die at all!'

'Well, *I'm* not going to,' he agreed, 'but one of us has to, and that leaves you. Otherwise I don't get my expenses for the journey home.'

This seemed to me a pretty feeble motive for murder, and I said so; but there was obviously no reasoning with a man like that, who fancied, moreover, that he had some sort of grudge against me.

So we delivered the *'morituri'* line more or less in unison – and I must say it was very well received, considering they must all have heard it often enough before – and I was wondering what to do next, when Nero bellowed pettishly, 'All right, all right, get on with it then!'

Actually, I don't think Delos can have heard him, because he went on acknowledging the applause, but I decided to take it as my cue for action. Because, look here, I wouldn't normally wish to take an unfair advantage, but I inspected my bruised fingers, and thought, 'Well, if that's the way he wants it, he can have it!'; and approaching him from the rear I threw my net completely over his enormous bulk, effectively entangling his ankles, and bringing him to the sawdust with an earth-shattering crash, and a rather vulgar oath.

Mind you, this didn't go down at all well with the crowd, which booed offensively; but I ask you to remember, Headmaster, that I could, had I so chosen, have used my javelin at this juncture, and that would have seen the end of the matter.

In fact, a moment later, I wished that I had done; for, on my asking him, somewhat prematurely perhaps, if he now yielded, he ignored the question completely, and lumbered dumbly to his knees, simultaneously drawing a nasty-looking broad-sword from its scabbard, with which he proceeded to hack at the all-enveloping mesh.

Well, no net was ever woven which could stand that sort of treatment for long, so I reluctantly hefted my main armament preparatory to a pre-emptive strike.

I say 'reluctantly' because I had no wish to injure the man, and until this very last minute had continued to hope that we might have arrived at some sort of rapprochement whereby we could turn on our captors, and emerge victorious. But no – the chances of such an accord now seemed to have receded irretrievably; so with a loud cry of 'Take that then, confound you!', I launched the weapon in the direction of my erstwhile companion's muscular midriff. Wherefrom it might well have bounced, for all I know; but unfortunately I had failed to notice that I was standing on a corner of the net, which my struggling adversary – whether intentionally or not, I cannot be sure – now pulled from beneath me, at the very instant that the missile left my hand, effectively spoiling my aim.

Even as I fell flat on my back, I watched appalled, as the javelin's deadly trajectory span sparkling in the morning sun to a target area some two inches to the left of Nero's ear, where it stuck, vibrating like a metronome, in the woodwork of the Royal Box.

There was a moment's silence, during which Delos muttered, 'Well, you've *really* done it now, haven't you?'; and then the Emperor squealed to his feet, advancing as his theory that treachery was at work, and that any right-thinking members of the public would do very nicely for themselves if they finished off the pair of us, thereby showing their loyalty to the throne and their allegiance to the established order of things, the . . . what's the phrase he used? . . . the *status quo*, that's it.

He and the rest of his party then disappeared down a sort of hatchway without bothering to stay for the sequel; which was that a murmuring mob of public spirited citizens, intent on adopting his recommendation *in toto*, leaped into the arena and sped towards us, whilst I hurriedly helped Delos divest himself of the rest of the reticulum, feeling that surely he must at last realise where his best interests lay, and stand beside me in this moment of crisis.

I then realised that the mob in question had stopped in its tracks for some reason, and was now sprinting right back where it came from; and looking round I discovered that, to add to our pleasure on this merry morning, some fool had let the lions out!

At the moment they were in mute pursuit of a bizarre figure in the dishevelled uniform of a member of the armed forces, who – absurdly, I thought, under the circumstances – was making shoo-ing gestures at them with a broken lyre; whereas everyone knows that you really need a chair for that sort of thing.

But it was not time to argue over the various techniques of animal training; and, united once more, Delos and I joined the flying fugitive as he traversed the arena, and leaped the barricade at the far side, opposition melting before us, in view presumably of our huge pursuers; and finally, in a last burst of speed we passed through the turnstiles to seek anonymity and safety in the streets of Rome!

Later: I have been trying to explain to Delos that it is now necessary for us to go *back* to the palace and rescue Barbara, but he does not seem to see it my way, and refuses to do anything of the sort!

What a strangely ungrateful man he is to adopt this attitude, after all I have done for him these past days! But no – he intends, he says, to return to Greece forthwith, and still grumbles about losing his expenses!

Very well, then: as usual I shall have to go on alone . . .

DOCUMENT XXVI

Seventh Extract from the Doctor's Diary

I did not linger long enough to witness the outcome of my inadvertent animal liberation movement, feeling that the entry of the great cats might well lead to the exit of the gladiators; and therefore the disruption of a sporting event to which Nero had evidently been looking greatly forward. And I had no wish to incur his odium just when it seemed we were getting on so well together.

As to the wretched assassin, I am not, I hope, a vindictive man, but I confess that the thought of his probable fate did not stir me to other than a chuckle. He had been asking for something of the sort ever since I left Assissium; and, as it is well known, malefactors trifle with me at their peril!

However, one consequence of the unfortunate fiasco did disturb me, for my lyre was manifestly unfit now for further service, and my revolutionary recital, which I had been anticipating pleasurably – albeit with a touch of that apprehension inseparable from public appearances – would now have to be cancelled *sine die*.

I therefore allowed a sufficient interval for tempers to cool, and then presented myself at the state apartments to make my excuses . . .

Nero, I thought, received me with less enthusiasm than is customary when fellow artistes foregather; but this was explained to my satisfaction when he told me he had once more narrowly escaped death at the hands of a malcontent; and I said that *there* was a coincidence, and it was small wonder that young people were no longer taking up music as a serious career, considering the occupational risks involved.

Speaking of which, I very much regretted that I would be unable to give my promised concert at his banquet that evening, as my particular and apparently personal assailant had got away with the lute. (That was a pleasantry which failed to raise a smile; probably because, as I later realised on reviewing the conversation, the lute was an instrument which first appeared in Europe during the fourteenth century – and loot as a synonym for booty was hardly in general use until the Capone era. Such are the conversational hazards of time-travel!)

I therefore rephrased the statement; and was more than slightly chagrined to receive no expression of sympathy or disappointment at my unfortunate dilemma, not even a consolatory 'Tut!'

How would Yehudi Menuhin have felt, I wondered, if on telling his promoter to cancel everything because he had carelessly sat on his Stradivarius, the man had merely raised an eyebrow, and said 'Well, well – these things happen . . . '?

No, so far as I could read the fluorescent features before me, they seemed to indicate a mild relief, if anything – a phenomenon I was at a loss to explain!

'You mean,' he enquired slowly, 'that there is absolutely no danger of . . . I mean, that we are definitely not to have the . . . the pleasure of hearing you perform? Poppy *will* be disappointed . . . I expect.'

I said I was glad *someone* would be; because the loss of my lyre meant the tragic curtailment of what could have been a brilliant career as a virtuoso.

'Do I understand then, that you intend *never* to play again? Not under any circumstances . . . whatever?'

'Well, I don't really see how I can . . . ' I told him; and then a really brilliant idea struck me: 'Unless, of course, you would care to lend me your own instrument for the evening?'

He shuddered for some reason; and then replied that it was quite out of the question, since it was a creation of exquisite workmanship, believed once to have been the property of Orpheus. And on the evidence of my behaviour to date – I cannot imagine what he meant by that! – he was afraid I might drop it.

'No,' he continued, strumming vaguely on the gem-encrusted artefact, 'as you say, it is indeed a sad loss to Music; but, on the other hand, of course, looking on the bright side, it does mean that I needn't after all, have you put to . . . put to any inconvenience; or see you torn apart . . . or torn apart by conflicting emotions, doesn't it? So now, I take it, you'll be returning to Corinth as soon as convenient, eh?'

I agreed that it was my intention to leave Rome, just as soon as we had completed our discussion concerning his municipal building programme, as provisionally pencilled onto the adenda of the agenda yesterday.

A harmless enough proposition, one would have thought. But strangely, he leaped to his feet, and screamed irritably, 'I suppose you think I haven't got one, don't you? People seem to imagine that I do simply nothing all day, but sit around writing songs, and persecuting Christians, and organising orgies, and all that . . .'

'And all what?' I asked him.

'That,' he replied evasively. 'But I tell you, there's a lot more to being an Emperor than you might suppose. There's . . . well, there's caring and concern, and so on. And . . . ah, yes . . . what about this? I have just received – look here! – the final winning entries for my 'Design a Capitoline' competition from the Institute of Architects! There you are – how about that?'

He had produced, during the above, a sheaf of plans from a drawer in the ormolu-encrusted sarcophagus between us, and flung them triumphantly onto the table. 'These'll lead to a fine old song and dance from the conservation lobby, wouldn't you say? Progressive as all get out, they are! Make Rome absolutely unrecognisable in no time at all!'

I must admit that the plans appeared to be a most impressive example of featureless urban sprawl; and I produced my spectacles with the multi-focal lenses, the better to examine the more soul-destroying, habitat flattering details of his projected Rome New Town

Conurbation; for I am, of course, a qualified architect myself, and could, I believe, have produced some distinguished work in that field, had I so chosen.

It was while I was thus engaged that Poppea entered the room, followed by a forlorn figure, which, through the high magnification of my glasses, I could have sworn was that of Barbara Wright! Startled out of my normal composure, I therefore removed the delusory pince-nez, laying them carefully on the blue-prints, and regarded the lady again from several angles, with the naked eye.

There could, incredibly, be no mistake!

It was the popular history mistress of Coal Hill Comprehensive, whom I had left safe in Assissium only two days ago!

DOCUMENT XXVII

Sixth Letter from Legionary (Second Class) Ascaris

Locusta,

You can hardly be surprised, I should think, that on this occasion I offer no terms of endearment or assurances of filial affection, as, where you are concerned, I find I am fresh out of same, owing to not hearing from you of late amongst other things, when, if ever, I have so sorely needed a mother's guiding fist in my predicaments.

For my part, I have never hesitated to send you such news of my doings as I hoped would have been of some interest, even to a seamier citizen than you (if ever there was one, but obviously there isn't).

So, all right then, if that is your attitude it will be the last of them I promise you, as I have now done with being dutiful, and in any case am leaving Rome on account of lions, with which circumstance I will not detain you owing to obvious lack of parental concern for such matters; and anyway, I have my hands full enough of the beasts for the moment, thank you – or will have if they can work out how to get down a manhole. Oh, how they do so snarl and salivate down my grating!

But enough of that for now, as I would not wish to bore you further with my humdrum life-style, and if spared shall be gone by dusk to begin a new one in some corner of a foreign field if I can find it, and be myself again, which is,

Ascaris.

DOCUMENT XXVIII

Third Selection of Jottings from Nero's Scrapbook

I do not think it could ever be said of me that I am an emperor to harbour a grudge, but I am beginning to dislike Maximus Petullian very much indeed.

I believe I have already made it clear in the privacy of these pages that my feelings towards Barbara are such as to set my soul soaring to Parnassus where it writes a good deal on the subject; and I am not, therefore, apt to be pipped at the post by some rube of a troubador, however retired he may claim to be, especially when he is three times my age, twice as mad, and half as talented! It's just not on!

So you can imagine my feelings when – deep in a succinct summary of my slum clearance project for Greater Rome – I realised I had lost his attention, and he was roguishly ogling my fair betrayer from every possible angle!

Furthermore, it was at once clear that she returned his interest, the baggage; for, with a loud cry, she dropped Poppy's shopping, and flopped sobbing at the fellow's feet, whence she addressed him as 'Doctor' –

obviously a barbarian term of endearment – causing him to splutter: 'Shush!'

It was clear to me, therefore, that they had met before, and moreover on terms of some intimacy; and I was about to demand an explanation with menaces, when a smell of burning distracted me from my catechism; and I discovered to my horror that my architectural extravagance, the working drawings on the basis of which the new Neropolis was to be constructed, were now slowly smouldering!

The reason for this was not at once apparent, and I was at a loss to account for the phenomenon; until Petullian interrupted my cries of ungovernable fury with an utterly inadequate 'Dear me!', detached himself from Barbara's embraces, approached the conflagration, and extracted therefrom the charred remains of an apparatus which it has been his occasional habit to balance on his nose! I had never stooped to enquire the cause of this one additional eccentricity amongst so many; but he now explained that it was an optical device intended to assist the eyesight, but he greatly feared it had now so concentrated the rays of the sun onto the parchment as to . . . well, he was sorry, but I could see what had happened, couldn't I? Just one of those unfortunate things!

I was in the process of taking the in-breath necessary for a prolonged tirade, when two lions entered the room, nodded casually, and curled up on the carpet.

Whereupon Petullian, rather in the manner of a prisoner in the dock asking for sixteen other offences to be taken into consideration, said that he would like to apologise for having let them out!

And after that events became somewhat confused, and conversation inarticulate, as we all made our own arrangements for the immediate future . . .

DOCUMENT XXIX

Eighth Extract from the Doctor's Diary

It is perhaps fortunate that the lions made their entrance when they did, for in another moment it is possible that Nero might have been inspired by the fortuitous inferno to initiate the burning of the city itself; a tragedy, had it really occurred, for which I would have had no wish to be held responsible, however indirectly.

Moreover, they created a useful diversion which enabled Barbara and me to leave the now chaotic throne-room, where the royal couple were clinging sloth-like to the chandeliers, and screaming for assistance.

I felt it best to take with us both the scorched plans *and* the imperial lyre, so that the obvious myth of Nero having 'fiddled' during the fictitious fire should have no possible foundation in fact.

As we were traversing the entrance hall with these trophies, whom should we encounter but Ian Chesterton on his way in, absurdly dressed as a gladiator! I rebuked both the latter and Barbara for having disobeyed my instructions and gone gallivanting on their own, for they might well have encountered serious trouble without the benefit of my experience and supervision.

At this, they seemed amused for some reason; and I decided that, in the face of this dawning irresponsibility, my best plan would be to curtail my holiday, collect Vicki from our hotel, and return to Assissium, before something serious occurred to any of my protegées.

Before doing so, however, it occurred to me that it might well benefit posterity if I were to complete the destruction of Nero's grey and grandiose scheme for the featureless construction of Rome, and perhaps therefore contribute, however slightly, to the sum of human happiness.

I therefore ignited once more the remains of the parchment and disposed of them down a sewer grating outside the Temple of Minerva.

At once there was a muffled explosion – presumably a pocket of methane gas had proved combustible – and out of a man-hole cover down the street emerged the familiar squat form of my regular assailant, attempting to beat out the flames on his tunic, as he fled once more into the gathering dusk. Well, let *that* be a lesson to him not to attack inoffensive tourists!

As we left the city I looked back and drew the attention of my three companions to a really splendid sunset. So bright were the colours that it almost looked as if the entire town were ablaze; and so magnificent was the spectacle that I could not forbear to salute the apparent conflagration with a farewell performance of

Thermodynamic Functions on Nero's lyre . . .

They looked at me strangely, with expressions that in the flickering red light seemed oddly horrified . . .

Well, it has been a pleasantly relaxing and instructive visit.

Ave atque vale!

EPILOGUE

A Second Epistle to
The Keeper of the Imperial Archives, Rome

Oh, my dear Sir!

Can it be – may I ask – that you at last bask in the light of my remarks, and are warmed by the dawning of comprehension, however minimal?

The letter with which you have the amazing grace to cover the return of the documents in what we may call, for convenience, the '*Quo Vadis*, TARDIS?' affair (yes, we may), encourages me to suppose so; and I therefore take a certain amount of grudging pleasure in honouring you with a few fruits of my own later speculations upon them.

Now, first of all, it would seem that Nero was eminently sensible – no matter what his motives may have been – to secure the assassination of the real Maximus Petullian; for, as my recent researches have confirmed, he was not only a singer of subversive social-protest material, but a radical agitator whose sole purpose in visiting Italy was to secure the re-establishment of the Republic.

Moreover, the loathsome Tavius, who fortunately

makes only a brief appearance in this chronicle, was just such another revolutionary, whose only motivation – beneath the 'cover' of honest slave gatherer! – was to open the floodgates of chaos to Democracy and Christianity, with all their attendant dissensions: and hence his jubilation at the death of the anonymous centurion, who, it seems, was head of Counter Intelligence.

The mysterious Doctor was, therefore, entirely correct to have no truck with the traitorous fellow, and his instincts were of the soundest when he expressed his determination not to become involved in any form of conspiracy which might conceivably lead to the Overthrow of Empire and the Downfall of Civilisation. In fact, his non-interventionist attitude, as revealed in the diary (which he later left, presumably inadvertently, on the kitchen table in Assissium, together with Chesterton's Journal, which he had apparently confiscated for its hyper-critical content) deserves nothing but praise.

We have to set against this, however, the fact that he first of all introduced the concept of atonal composition to Roman music; then released several lions into the streets of Rome; and, finally, accidentally set fire to that city; and these matters can hardly be overlooked – especially since Nero was subsequently blamed for all of them, proclaimed a public enemy by the Senate, and driven to his death; which, in retrospect, can only seem a very unfortunate misunderstanding!

Now, since this misunderstanding is the primary basis for the claims to the Imperial Purple of Emperors

Galba, Otho, Vespasian, Trajan (the well-known columnist), and our current genial incumbent, Hadrian (whom Jupiter preserve), you will perhaps understand why I have been hesitant to bring the somewhat embarrassing circumstances of his legally unsound position before the Emperor.

He is not a man prone to brook criticism lightly; and, in any case, it is a bit late now for anyone to do anything at all about it, so it is my considered inclination to let the matter drop.

I would, in fact, suggest that all the relevant papers be covered by the Official Secrets Act; and not released, if at all, until, let us say, the year 1987 . . .

However, should your bureaucratic bigotry lead you not to share my reticence, then I have one suggestion to make which might be of some assistance.

I hear from my father-in-law, General Agricola, that the building of Hadrian's projected wall is being hampered by the presence in the construction team of Legionary (now Fourth Class) Ascaris!

Supposing, therefore, that he were to be recalled to Rome to face various charges arising from his indiscreet correspondence, so sensibly handed to me by his mother, Locusta, in return for instant cash . . . Then he could well be made to seem responsible for the whole ghastly fiasco, our problem would be neatly resolved, and I could remain, for the foreseeable future,

    Your relieved historian,
                  Tacitus.

Post Scriptum: In view of all the circumstances, may I now look forward with confidence to receiving your cheque by return of post?

T.